I0580856

Für Elyse

"I never thought I'd love anyone so much…"

The Gryphon & The Lyre

by

Elliott Milstein

Cover Design: Maggie Spurgeon
Illustrations: Benard Okoremu

Published in the United States
Mystic Canyon Publishing, LLC

The Gryphon and the Lyre
ISBN: 978-1-958411-11-7

Table of Contents

The Gryphon

LABORERS

The Lyre

SUITES

LABORERS

First Job

August 13, 1982

I been canned lotsa times. Nothin' wrong wit' gettin' fired, ya know. It's just how it goes sometimes. I was once fired over a pickle. True story! My first job, too, actually.

So, this was the summer of, what, eighty-one or eighty-two? I was, wait, sixteen I guess, yeah, I just got my driver's license so, yeah, eighty-two it was. It was my buddy Jeff hooked me up wit' that job in the mall. Jeff, great guy, ya know. We had a blast workin' there together, lemme tell you. Good times, good times.

It was Burger Chef. No, not Burger King, Burger *Chef.* Yes, there really was a Burger Chef and believe you me, their burgers were better. Better than Burger King, better than McDonald's, no lie. So, here's the story.

Jeff and I were buds at school. Nah, he wasn't a *paisan*, but still a good guy. We hung out, got stoned together, stuff like that…

C'mon! So what! The kid's sixteen, he's old enough. Probably smoked some grass himself already, haven't ya, kid? Jeez! Is that what you were fired for? No?

Whaddya mean, "disrespect"? The old man's not here, okay? He's dead. Remember? Hey kid, no disrespect to Nonno, okay, just telling a story. Hey, he was my dad too, ya know. Don't youse worry about me corruptin' your little boy, Jimmy. He's older than you think.

C'mere, kid. Grab me a brewsky and we'll go in the den. I'll meet you there. Hey, pssst. Make it two.

Hey, sis, whaddya doing in here all alone? Hey, hey, little girl. C'mon. He had a good long life, ya know. Life wasn't easy for him, working two jobs most his life. I know that, ya know. C'mon, cheer up. I know no one's s'pose to be cheery at a *Veglia funebre*, but *Madone*! Like Father Michael said, "A better place," ya know. The old man was a fighter to the end, wasn't he though? Tough old guy, workin' the dockyards wit' them Pollacks and Micks. He had to be, didn' he? Time to rest, ya know. Well, you know what they say…

Hey, kid, thanks. Siddown. Aunt Gina's here but she won't mind. I'm telling him the story 'bout how I got fired from Burger Chef. No,

Chef not King. Jesus H. Christ, don't nobody remember nothin'? You were just a kid, though. Probably don't remember. Anyways, if youse don't remember, you'll like this too.

Siddown, kid. So, here, lemme tell ya. So, Jeff, he gets this after-school gig over at the mall, right? 'Cause, ya know, he already got his license—lucky bastard—and the mall's way too far to hoof it or even grab the bus. Me? I gotta wait till I get mine, but soon as I do? Bam! Jeff hooks me up wit' a job there too.

Man, we had a friggin' blast, just hangin' out at the mall, doin' our thing. True story! We were workin' in the food court, so it wasn't just us, ya know? We were always hangin' wit' the other kids workin' at the joints around us. Like, what was that one place? Orange Julius, right! Remember those, Ginny? Or that pretzel spot—what the hell was the name? And oh, Cinnabon. Forget about it, I loved that place. Partly 'cause, ya know, the buns were killer, but also, there was this chick workin' there—damn, what was her name? Anyway, she was somethin' else, lemme tell ya. Had a rack on her could stop traffic.

Aw, c'mon, Ginny, not you, too. He's fuckin' sixteen, you don't think he notices girls' tits? Look, he's blushing, can you believe it? Awww, c'mon Billy, just messin' wit' ya.

Anyways, so get this—lunch and dinner times? Forget about it, it was always slammed. But we'd stay open till the mall shut down, like 10 o'clock or somethin', and by then, it wasn't that busy, so, ya know, we'd mess around a little.

Brad, the manager, he'd dip out around eight most nights, so it'd just be me and Jeff, and then there was this other guy, Vargie. His real name was Mark Vargus, but we called him Vargie. Total loser, lazy as hell. I swear, Jeff and me, we did all the work while this guy just coasted.

And then there was Stacey. She only worked like two three days a week—I think it was 'cause she had dance class or somethin'. She was real cute, but, eh, I was too much of a chicken to make a move, ya know?

Alright, so lemme tell ya, this one night in August—it sticks out 'cause it was near the end of summer, and by then, it was like, who gave a shit what we did? We'd goof off a lot at night, ya know? So, it's about closing time, the place is dead, the mall's practically empty, and we're just messin' around wit' the food. I mean, half that stuff's gettin' tossed anyway, right? And yeah, we used to munch on it, too. What can I say? We were kids, we were hungry.

So, we're foolin' around, and we start this little food fight — everyone did it, it wasn't just us, no lie. So, I grab this pickle, right? And I'm aiming it at Jeff, but the asshole ducks, and bam! That sucker goes flyin' over the counter and smacks this dude square in the chest. Guy's wearin' a suit an' everything, probably comin' back from a show or somethin'. He's got a lady wit' him – I barely noticed her, 'cause I'm sweatin' what this guy's gonna say.

And man, he flips out. Total asshole, makin' a scene over nothin'. Like, come on, it's a friggin' pickle, didn't even leave a mark! But he's yellin', and Matt — he was like an assistant manager or somethin' — steps in and says, "Hey, whatever you guys want, it's on the house." That shuts the guy up, so he and his girl eat their burgers and Cokes or whatever, and we think that's the end of it.

But nah, not really. Turns out we forgot about the damn security cams. Either that or somethin' didn't add up wit' the register 'cause we didn't ring up their food. I dunno. Anyway, Brad, the manager, he tears into me the next day, cussin' me out left and right. And just like that, bam! I'm outta there. Jeff tried to stick up for me, and even Vargie — lazy-ass Vargie — he backs me up, sayin' we all did it. But the camera? Nah, it just caught me, so that was that.

Whatever, man. Screw that job anyway. School was startin' in a week or so, so it's not like I was gonna be workin' there much longer. But boy, did Pop lose it when he found out. Pretty sure I got the belt that night — hard to remember, though. I got the belt so much it all kinda blends together.

Nah, Ginny, you didn't get it, I know. But you ask Jimmy or Tony – they got their share. Maybe not as much as me, but they got it. Your Nonno? Oh, he was all sweet and playful wit' you kids, but wit' us? Forget about it. Guy was tough as nails, rode us hard. No lie. Well, it took wit' your dad, alright, and Uncle Tony, but I was a stupid ass, so it took me a little longer.

The next summer, I got a job at 'Sbarro in the same mall. Actually, it was in the exact same spot as the Burger Chef, which was outta business by then. Serve them fuckin' right. And now I got Jeff the job at 'Sbarro. Nothin' much happened that summer. We were graduatin' anyway. Tony was already in law school I think, and your dad was jus' startin' high school. Maybe I got him a job too, I think. I'll ask him. HEY JIMMY, YOU LITTLE FUCK, GET IN HERE AND BRING ME A BEER! Jeez.

I don't think he heard me. Ginny, you mind gettin' him for me? No, I'm not drunk. Pop would want us reminiscin' ya know. Ma's in the kitchen I think. Hey, Jimmy! You bring my beer? Never mind. Still talking 'bout the old days wit' Billie here. When I worked at 'Sbarro summer of '83 you were goin' into tenth grade, I think. Where'd ya work that summer? Union Tires? Are you fuckin' me? Never mind, I didn't think you… Freddo got you that job? Fuck, I didn't work there till… shit, I can't remember exactly.

Lemme see, after graduation I got the job at Honest Ed's. Used cars, man. What a racket. That old fuckin' Jew made a fuckin' fortune there. I hated that job, man. But I stuck wit' it. Then Uncle Sonny got me the job at Union Tires…

Minga!, you wanna bring that shit up. But that was after Union, I think. No, you're right, it was before. Or at the same time, I think.

Alright, kid, I'll tell ya, but it ain't exactly my proudest moment, ya know? I used to work for Shelly the Safe Man. Nah, I didn't carry the cash or nothin' – I just ran the numbers. That's it. True story, I swear. I had nothin' to do wit' the other stuff. But, ya know, things got hot, the Shell got pinched, and I had to lay low, so I lit out to California for a while to let things cool down.

I'll tell ya, Cali was somethin' else. Sun shinin' every day, warm weather, and beautiful broads everywhere. True story. I mean, man, I had my fun out there, lemme tell ya. Alright, alright, I ain't gonna get into it. But it was the fuckin' nineties, ya know? Things were poppin' out there, good times all around, no lie. But I had a few jobs there. Yeah, canned a couple times, but more times I just walked off. They were all bullshit jobs anyway.

But yeah, then nine-eleven happened, and that kinda shook things up, ya know? I decided it was time to come back home. We lost some good people, real good *cugines*. Joey, Michael, Walter... all Ma's side of the family, ya know, union guys, firefighters. You knew that, right, Billie? All the *cugines* from Nonna's side were wit' the fire department. Why they couldn't find somethin' for me, I don't know. Maybe they didn't like Pop too much.

I mean, come on, Ginny, where were they, huh? You see 'em there today? At Pop's funeral? Nothin'! *Vaffanculo*, I say. It would've been nice if they looked out for family a little, ya know?

But nah, you guys are doin' fine. Tony's a big-shot lawyer now, and your Pop – hey, where the hell he go? – yeah, your Pop's Mr. Wall Street, makin' millions. But hey, sunshine don't last forever. I always say, wait for the rain. Golden parachute? More like a golden shower, you ask me. *Fungool!* The world's a fuckin' mess.

Con Ed, Gina? Really? What, you think I was gonna work for Con Ed, spend my life crawlin' through fuckin' sewers all day? Thanks, Uncle Freddo, but… no. Get the fuck outta here.

Anyways, Uncle Val hooked me up wit' the gig at Ferraro's when I got back, and I been there, what, six seven years now? It's been good. Started as the valet, just bringin' cars around, but old man Ferraro, he kinda took me under his wing. Alright, alright, more like he kicked my ass – Pop probably told him to – but it worked, ya know? Straightened me out. Now I'm up front, sellin' cars. I hit quota most months, and I been Salesman of the Month more times than I can count. True story!

It's that Italian charm, kid. The broads, they eat it up. So yeah, all's good now. Life's alright. So, no, kid, getting' canned ain't the end of everythin', no matter what your old man says.

But, yeah, Ginny, it was a rougher road for me than for you guys. I was the middle boy, ya know. And, you, yeah, our beautiful little baby girl, who could do no wrong. But me! Shit, it was always the belt, man. Always that fuckin' belt. But maybe I needed it. Maybe if he'd hit me a few more times I never woulda thrown that pickle. No lie!

A Night to Remember

December 31, 1979

Memory, that fragile protean faculty, haunts the rooms of one's mind like a timorous lodger in a house long inhabited yet oddly unfamiliar. It drapes itself in veils of shadow, revealing its treasures only rarely in bold pronouncements but more frequently in enigmatic whispers. One may seek it earnestly, hoping to grasp the precise image of a moment, yet, like moonlight glitter on a darkling lake, it alters with every effort to capture it. The past, so seemingly fixed in time, reveals itself instead as fluid intimations, transformed by the rippling influence of all that came after. In that labile landscape of reverie, one finds oneself suspended, neither wholly in the present nor entirely in the past, but caught in that liminal space where the self is both actor in and spectator of the event. What once appeared bright and defined becomes, in retrospect, softened, clouded, murky, its colors withered by later experience, its edges blurred by the brazen hand of emotion, its substance thinned by wasted time. Thus, most memories dissolve into a faint essence, or even stark nothingness, while a precious few coalesce into an adamantine brilliance such that the whole of one's life is reduced to a few raisins of crystal clarity in a vast bowl of the mushy gruel of vague impressions; yet even those so enshrined, bursting forth with startling lucidity, rich in texture, alive with sensation, are frequently distorted as well, evoking a remembrance of unsure verity.

Children live in a perpetual *now.* Their unaccustomed minds lack the capacity for contemplation of the future, and there is, for them, simply too little past on which to dwell. The child may reflect on what happened yesterday, or even the previous week, and they might plan events for tomorrow or the upcoming weekend, but that period of time is so short in duration for the adult, who, looking back decades, might well consider it all as the *present.* The child rises from bed, performs morning lavation, dresses, and proceeds to the breakfast table where eggs and toast and cereal and orange juice await, without once considering who had to make that breakfast, who had to shop for those groceries, or whose labor paid for it. No. Down goes all that nourishing food, and out the door to school or adventure the child shoots. It is around the middle of high school, I suppose, that one begins to consider a broader future because college looms and all that that entails: where to go, what to major in, and what to be in "the real world" where one must grapple with work, responsibilities, and other grown-up things. Especially sex.

At least that's what, harking back from a rather distant vantage point, I recollect it felt like in my middle-class Jewish life in suburban Detroit in the 1970's. Whilst the reflections of most childhood activities remain dim and hazy, if they can be recalled at all, with the kindling of the libido and the emerging outsized importance of girls, early adolescent interest in the distaff half of the schoolroom fired rapidly into an all-consuming obsession and a burning desire for sex, to the point where I can hardly educe much of those three frenetic years, except the girls; every girl with whom I had had even a passing fancy is illumined clearly while many male acquaintances from class or sports arise in my mind's eye merely as foggy apparitions.

After a year of fumbling about as a freshman, I emerged sophomore year – and especially as a junior once I made the basketball team – a bit of a lady's man. Beth and Sherry were early puppy romances, barely sliding into first base (to descend to the argot of that age), but things grew much more serious with Marilyn, Shirley, Janet, and Andee, with whom I hit regular doubles and the occasional triple.

My high school career ended on a damp squib, however, when I failed to make much time with my prom date, Susie Kellerman, despite that evening's expense of a corsage, a tux, a limousine, a hotel room, a bottle of champagne and a joint of prodigious authority. Prom itself is a complete blur, suffused with the white-hot flame of my passion and the atramentous disappointment of its utter failure. Whether I had had enough of a good time with Susie to warrant the invitation being extended yet again for graduation night, or I was motivated by the need to correct the washout of prom, I cannot at the moment recall, but I remember clearly walking with her on our school's second floor, not far from my locker, and asking her to meet up at Paul Cohen's house after the celebrations downtown. Funny, though, that all I recall of graduation night itself was hitting a homer with Stacey.

Matriculation at Northwestern broadened my horizons, not only intellectually, but socially as well. Everyone I knew was going to either the University of Michigan or Michigan State, with a few outliers, like me, one of whom went to Harvard and another to Oberlin. Being dropped by my parents in Evanston at the tender age of eighteen was quite frightening, with all the intimidation of being alone in a congregation of such scholars, but friends were made quickly, and girls came almost as fast. In a bare eighteen months I managed three girlfriends and, by Christmas break of my sophomore year, was rather deep into a committed relationship with the third, Jane Cooley, whose exceptional beauty, not to mention sexual sophistication and prowess, erased nearly all recollections of Belinda and Bethany, my earlier romances, despite each of them having lasted a not inconsiderable amount of time, involving numerous dates, including, occasionally, an elaborate and expensive evening at Pete Miller's. Whilst the difference between a high school senior girl and college freshman woman may only be a few months, for some reason – perhaps the idea of being away from home, the need to score off some old boyfriend, or the loosening bonds created by much more access to alcohol – I found I could abandon the puerile baseline of adolescence in favor of a metaphor-free world, home runs having become the standard at-bat with no baseball imagery to describe what pleasures lay beyond home plate.

As we now approach the particular evening I wish to memorialize, the specific details required to fill out the story are lost or obfuscated in my own recollections, no matter how much time I spend searching those muddled or empty drawers of memory's file cabinet. I have thus reached out to friends and family to supply the critical missing data. In doing so, I found numerous conversational prompts dredging back some fragments, but just as frequently, the anamnesis of incidents and opinions of others striking a discordant note of unfamiliarity or contradiction, leading me to question, if not completely discard, a number of proffered reflections. This story is, therefore, a crazy patchwork quilt – some pristine remnants of personal memories, some the ragged recollections of others, and some an amalgam of the two – but the facts of the story about the night itself come from me alone and they are as accurate as any memory can be, clothed in images with the subtlety of recalled glances and conversations that replay in my mind with the mannerisms, expressions, inflections, and stumbling words of the moment.

I was home for the High Holidays and happened to run into Susie and her family at Temple, so she and I ended up spending time catching up during the Oneg on Rosh Hashanah. We were joined by several other friends from high school, when Paul mentioned that he was planning a New Year's Eve party, and we should all come.

"It'll be great," he said. "My parents are going to be out of town and we can party all night. Plenty of booze and weed and food and shit."

"Sure," said Susie immediately, as did her friend Denise, who always seemed to be around wherever Susie went. "You'll be there too, Danny?"

There seems to be a little confusion – or at least controversy – over what exactly happened next, but I remember clearly that Susie had somehow indicated to me that it would be very much worth my while to show up. Paul and Ken back me up on that, though there is a distinctly robust minority report, with Susie herself as principal author, that any suggestion of guaranteed sexual gratification was entirely self-delusional. I admit – and have always maintained – that Susie made no *definite* promise, but that the nature of that and subsequent conversations, including one phone call made during Christmas break, provided strong indication that my high school fantasies would finally be fulfilled.

All of which, from the current vantage, strikes me with the incongruity of an evening sunrise or salt in a sugar cube as I had already asked Jane to Homecoming, which we attended – and much more following that – even as I stayed in contact with Susie. With such a bright sexual career at Northwestern, and especially enjoying the magnificent ministrations of Ms. Jane, there was no reason for my hankering after Susie. Whilst I was a bit of a player, I did, even in my callow days, have enough moral alignment to remain monogamous. So, the recollection of feeling great ambivalence about meeting Susie at the party, with those tentative promises, given that things with Jane had heated to a significant temperature, remains consistent with the vivid sense that it would be illaudable to find myself New Year's Eve with one girl while still in a deep, intimate relationship elsewhere.

Which is how I ended up at my grandfather's house that night. I told Paul (and asked him to spread the word) that I was unable to attend the party because I had to spend the night with my grandfather. This excuse was launched as a deliberate lie, but I chose subsequently to alter course to ensure that it would be true. Paul was a little put out and Susie even more so, not just because I didn't attend the party, but also because I didn't bother to call her to tell her, allowing the knowledge to confront her unceremoniously when she arrived at Paul's home.

"I'm never going to speak to that asshole again," she said to Denise. And Denise, who never particularly cared for me, supported that decision. Paul and the guys were more understanding but still disappointed.

My grandfather, or Papa, or, as I liked to call him, "Pops," was an ancient man, much older than the grandparents of my friends, a nonagenarian at this point, in fact. I was the youngest child of a youngest child and that tends to put a lot of distance between grandparents and grandchildren. He was old for as long as I remember. I, therefore, fail to have the plethora of grandparental memories others hold dear despite his being my only surviving grandparent. But I was certainly close enough to invite myself over for New Year's Eve, and he was certainly thrilled to have me.

The temperature had taken a significant and sudden turn that week, especially New Year's Eve. Night lay upon the world with a merciless, unrelenting cold, a bitterness that crept into one's very bones. The air, keen as a blade, sliced the snow-clad streets with a vigorous insistence, sighing through the skeletal branches of trees long stripped of their leaves. It was a night not merely frigid but possessed of an exquisite severity, but inside Pops's bungalow, all was warm and snug.

I don't think either of us had any expectation of making it to midnight, but we watched the Dick Clark show anyway, Pops wishing Guy Lombardo was still alive, while munching popcorn and chatting during the commercials. I don't remember exactly how or why I decided to ask Pops about his childhood, but I think it flowed naturally from whatever we were discussing.

"I know you worked in the auto industry, Pops, but I don't think I know anything else about your early life. How did you come to America?"

He gave me a strange look, difficult to describe, but, closing my eyes, I can still see his face at that moment, so his expression was certainly unusual enough for it to have fixed so powerfully in my memory. Tilting his head slightly, he betrayed a fine, peculiarly ironic grin, where surprise, pleasure, and wonder were all wrapped up together. But what he said then was most surprising.

"Let's have a glass of schnapps."

I didn't know what schnapps was but, of course, I agreed. I now know what schnapps is, and we did not have it. "Schnapps," it turns out, in addition to being a distasteful German liqueur, is also the Yiddish word for just "whiskey". Now, I had done some drinking up at school, despite not quite reaching the age where such imbibing was legal, but it was always beer or Jungle Juice at some frat house. I'd had wine at Passover since I was fourteen, but straight hard liquor? No, that was new to me.

We walked the four feet from the living room with its plastic-covered sofa and chair into the small kitchen. It was a cheerful space, its walls painted a soft pastel – buttery yellow with flecks of mint green – complemented by bright linoleum flooring. A white enamel stove stood beside an old, humming Frigidaire, their chrome handles gleaming under the warm glow of a single overhead light. White Formica countertops, edged in shiny aluminum, framed a deep porcelain sink where dishes dried in a metal rack. In the corner was a small, Formica-topped table with two metal chairs with half backs.

He sat me down at the table, then ambled around in preparation, bringing, in succession, two small glasses of water, a plate of Ritz crackers, two shot glasses, and then, from the fridge, a well-chilled bottle of Old Grand Dad. He sat on the other side of the table, poured out the two shots, held his glass up, said "Le Chaim" and knocked it back. I said "Le Chaim" in return and drained mine just as I saw him do.

As my eyes began to clear, I saw him pouring another shot in each of our glasses. "You need a chaser. Have a cracker and a sip of vatter," he said. I did. And, again, "Le Chaim." Again, the chaser. Again, "Le Chaim." Well, you get the idea. I don't remember exactly how many shots we had that night, but I do remember most of the life story he told me between them.

He was born in 1887, in the village of Berdichev, the southern end of The Pale. They came to America after what was, evidently, a particularly malignant pogrom, but he could not quite recall the details. I was hoping for a story of seeing the Statue of Liberty, but he had no memory of that. The family settled in Providence, Rhode Island, so perhaps they didn't go through Ellis Island.

He was quickly apprenticed to an electrician, a trade his parents thought would prepare him for the future so he could move past being a pushcart peddler like his father. He was excited to learn a trade and earn his own money. In his last year as an apprentice, he and his "master" electrified a church for which he received a bonus of five dollars – a whole week's salary. Hearing there were good jobs in Detroit, this young man of eighteen, with coins jingling in his pocket, took the train west alone and disembarked at the transcendent train station on Michigan Avenue.

"I valked out into de future. I saw cars in Providence, but only vun or two, owned by de rich people. Most people valked or had a horse. Outside the station in Detroit, dere ver some horses, but mostly cars, going back and forth. I vill always remember it," he finished, closing his eyes to recall the precise image.

He found his way to an auto factory. In those days, the hiring agents would stand on boxes outside the factory gates and men looking for work would walk up and be interviewed, and then be waived in. At the end of the day, they were paid in cash – $2 a day, which was considered a pretty decent wage, even including the fact that it was a grueling 10-hour day.

"But I made more den dat!" he said proudly.

"How so?", I asked.

"Ven de man asked if I had a special skill, I told him I vuss an electrician apprentice. He said I vuss to report to de electroplating room, and I'd get $3 a day! And I didn't have to verk on de line!"

He never returned to Providence. Five dollars a week was a low, but acceptable wage; tripling that was wealth beyond imagination. He rented a room but soon could afford to purchase half a duplex. He bought a car. Then the rest of the duplex. Then he married my Nana.

Since my retirement, I have read several books on the history of Detroit, but none contained the details Pops gave me that evening. Detroit was growing fast and there was very little indoor plumbing. The public bathhouses were open to men on Mondays, Wednesdays, and Fridays, and to women on Tuesdays, Thursdays, and Saturdays. Sunday was split: women in the morning and men in the afternoon.

"But I bathed every day," he said with pride.

"You had indoor plumbing?" I asked.

"No, but I vuss an auto verker and vee had showers in de plant."

No book I've read provided that information.

He described the city physically, what it was like to live there, watching the rapid transition from horse to automobile, the inclusion of indoor plumbing, the streetcars and buses, and the widening of Woodward Avenue. It was not unlike how I would later describe the advent of computers, cell phones, and the internet with the explosion of Silicon Valley.

He was laid off during the Great Depression. "But I verked every day." By this time, part of the Providence family had followed him, including his parents. Working his father's pushcart some days (declining to join his brother in the Purple Gang – that's another whole story), he would go to a downtown wholesaler and buy fruit and vegetables.

"Den I got the idea of selling things on de trains. I'd pick up some apples, ties, and playing cards and ride de train from Detroit to Chicago, peddling to de passengers. Playing cards ver de best, because they only vanted dem on de train, so dey vould leave de cards, and I vould pick 'em up and sell dem again."

As a Jew, he either couldn't or did not choose to work at Ford's. His first company was Olds Motor Works (later Oldsmobile) and then Hupmobile. After the Depression, he worked at Buick. During the war, he worked at a tank manufacturing plant, another cog in "the great arsenal of democracy." After that, he went into the tool-and-die business, hoping my dad or Uncle Max would join him, but that didn't come off for some reason. He sold the business to his workers when my older sister was born. He was already an old man by the time I arrived.

I never looked at my Papa the same way again. His face, to my juvenile perception, had presented itself as a mere arrangement of features, an assembly of lines and facets fixed in their indifferent symmetry. It was the mask of the unknown, the surface upon which his mind was hitherto a closed book, if I'd thought about him having a mind at all. But that rugged, wrinkled face, which at first had seemed a thing apart, began, by degrees, as he spoke and reminisced, revealing hitherto hidden tracts of his life, to move and transform. The contours softened into a new expression; the eyes, at first a cool abstraction, grew rich with history; the set of his mouth, which once seemed carved into a simple, benignant smile, now betrayed vistas of feeling; his demeanor, once of mere kindness, hardened into that of an old-time factory worker. A slight contraction of his brow no longer signified merely thought but *his* thought, not merely history but *his* history. His was no longer a face but a story, and not just his story, but the story of a city, an industry, a country. Even his accent seemed to soften. Where I once saw only an old man – true, an old man I loved and who loved me, but still, just an old man – I now saw a world.

He moved into an assisted living facility shortly after that. At least, he was living in one by the time I moved home. We had a big celebration when he turned one hundred, but he died shortly after that. I was with him in the hospital just a few hours before he left us. I asked him how he was feeling, and he said, "I'm going to die." I was about to mouth some silly platitude like, "Oh, no, you'll be fine," when I stopped myself, realizing what a stupid thing that was to say to a centenarian, and asked instead, "How do you feel about that?"

"I got no kicks," he said. "I had a good life. All my brothers and sisters are gone. Everyone I know is gone. It's time. Yes. It's time." I kissed him and said good night. He passed around 2 am: "his eye had not dimmed, nor his natural force abated."

Susie, my high school sweetheart who was, by this time, my wife, was very supportive throughout the whole process, especially as she and Pops became quite close, despite his having provided me the alibi for not seeing her that New Year's Eve. Susie is unable to recall – or unwilling to share – the moment she recognized that friendship had, for her, blossomed into true love, but I think, for me, it began that evening, by eschewing the path of personal gratification and finding, in its place, a connection with history – the world's as well as my own – through an evening of reminiscence about a young man of my age moving through a world removed from mine, not just in time, but in substance as well, with a capability I found as admirable as it was revelatory.

If youth, in its fervid heedlessness, exults in the mere rapture of sensation, maturity, tempered by reflection and modesty, learns to enfold passion within the richer, more enduring fabric of love. It is not that desire is wholly effaced – rather, it is refined, its edges softened, its demands subsumed into a deeper, more knowing comprehension of the other. Where once attraction was a reckless impulse, suffused with the urgency of lust, it becomes, with time and reflection, an attachment warm, bright, and tenacious, enriched by memory and strengthened by constancy.

And so, I would say later, love for Susie came to me, unknowingly, as I learned to love my grandfather in a new, tender way. Perhaps not entirely true, but I know I returned to Evanston a different person. I broke up with Jane soon after and even changed my major from Poli Sci to Economics. I know that, by graduation, when I planned to move back to Detroit, I was not moving for a job or graduate school, nor to be close to family or Pops or friends, nor to return to the familiar city of my youth, but to be with Susie. She had settled there, and I wanted to settle wherever she was.

Would Susie and I have ended up together had I gone to that New Year's party? Counterfactual histories are notoriously capricious, making such speculations specious, but I suspect not. I almost certainly would have ruined the evening with some brash and graceless overture, and I am equally sure that whatever would have subsequently occurred, the memory of that party would have dissipated, whilst my reflections on that night with Pops are enshrined in a clear, immutable, defined and cherished vision.

To this day I keep a bottle of Old Grand Dad in my fridge from which I drink a shot or two – no chaser – once a year, on my grandfather's *Yahrzeit*, as I recall that fated night of revelation and change and invoke his blessed memory.

Dumbo!

May 29, 1941

It was love at first sight.

I know that's a rather overly used, trite phrase to begin a story, but as it is the positively solemn truth and a great way to set the stage, I couldn't resist. I'm not really a writer – artist actually, as it happens – but I have this writer friend and when I told him I wanted to write this story but didn't know really how to begin it, he said I needed to "set the stage." He explained that he meant I should begin with something that tells the reader what the story is going to be about and also where and when it takes place. So now that you know what it's about, I shall attend to the particulars of when and where.

The story takes place in Hollywood, California in the year of 1941. But a little more background is warranted first, I think. For a number of years before that, I had been working at what was then the fledgling studio of Mr. Walt Disney – I started in 1938, shortly after they completed *Snow White and the Seven Dwarfs.* My family had gotten out of Austria in 1933, at the first whiff of Naziism next door, emigrating to the UK, but we only stayed there long enough for me to learn English. Then it was on to the United States. It wasn't easy for Jews to get into the US back then, but somehow my father found a way. I had been in art school in Vienna but never completed my studies. Fortunately, it was just enough experience to land a job at a design firm in New York. But when I heard that Disney was looking for animators, I made my way to LA post-chaise, where I got a job as an inbetweener.

It is not easy to explain the extremely intricate configurations of the various personnel of a Hollywood animation studio. Although I believe the system I will explain, putting it as briefly as I can ("get to the story as quickly as possible"), may have been unique to the Disney organization at the time of which I speak, I have heard that other studios have since adopted it. There are, essentially, different teams to handle different aspects of the film: one team will develop the characters, another the backgrounds, another special effects, and so on. But the main animators of each team only draw the first frame out of the twenty-four that make up one second of a movie. The twenty-three other frames – the ones that come in-between the main ones – are drawn by a team of animators known as "inbetweeners." Clever name. Supposedly Walt himself came up with it.

Inbetweening, or "tweening," as we called it, was really scraping the bottom of the bucket for an artist. It was exacting work, determining the perfect position of each slight movement of everything in each frame from number two to number twenty-four, but it was also pretty boring (though not as brain-numbing as the work the ink-and-paint girls had to do; but they weren't even technically "artists"). But there was always the hope of a promotion to a key animator position in backgrounds, sequencing, character design, or even art direction.

We worked on the ground floor of the Animation Building where we had our own desks, although they were rather close together, and it was quite noisy and raucous. Not like the upper floors where worked the great Art Davis, Ward Kimball, not to mention Walt himself. I got along with other inbetweeners pretty good – although some were put out by my accent and others by my religion – but the most lasting relationship I was to form in that giant drafting room was my friendship with Jared "Jerry" Mentnor.

Jerry started out in "serious art," as we liked to call it. A born New Yorker, it was natural he would find an art school there, but not a given thing necessarily that he would end up at the Art Students League, where he studied under the likes of Thomas Hart Benton, Kenneth Hayes Miller, and Reginald Marsh. Even with such credentials, he ended up the typical starving artist, *schlepping* his paintings from gallery to gallery, but with no luck. The gallery owners varied in size and shape, in age and experience, in religion and politics, in ethnicity and national origin, but in one thing they were in complete agreement: Mentnor paintings would never grace their walls.

Hearing of better opportunities out west and, still being a young man, he followed the advice of one of America's great newspaper editors to "go" there. The gallery owners in LA, while living in a sunnier ambience, did not seem to have any sunnier viewpoints towards his paintings, but one did recommend a job at Disney, and there he ended up, on a stool right next to mine. We quickly discovered numerous mutual interests, and if my accent or religion was any issue with him, he certainly never mentioned it. We fell into friendship with an immediacy that was, well, almost love at first sight. But that's not the love at first sight I was referring to when I began this story. And now, I suppose, it is time to get out with it.

The company was still in its rather cramped and rundown quarters on Hyperion Avenue when we met, but we all knew that they were building a giant 50-acre complex in Burbank, and we were thrilled to move there in early 1940, just as they were about to start work on the classic film, which I am sure you all seen with your children – *Dumbo!*

It was a difficult time, what with the war in Europe and the layoffs after the box office failures of *Pinocchio* and *Fantasia.* Ben Sharpsteen, our boss, told us money was cramped and that we had to keep things simple and inexpensive. We even went to inbetweening 12-frame instead of 24 to move things along, and we used watercolor for much of the background work, which speeded up the coloring process. There was a lot of dissatisfaction and union talk. I can even remember Walt giving a big speech to everyone to keep them working and non-union. I leaned more socialist than Jerry, but as a foreign guest at a difficult time, I kept my head down and contributed nothing to the union discussions.

Although we both missed our usual lunch hauntings on Hollywood Blvd. or the diner on Franklin when we worked near Griffith Park, we were generally very pleased with the bill of fare at the Disney commissary, where I typically lunched on a Prince Charming Hamburger, and Jerry would get outside a Sleeping Beauty Tuna Sandwich with a Jiminy Cricket Lemonade. The commissary, a modernistical, stream-lined room designed more for efficiency than esthetic appeal, had quickly become a social hub of the new digs, and employees were actually encouraged to linger and socialize. Walt liked the idea of the studio personnel as one big, happy family. During the union talk, he increased his visits there, which was quite nice, really, although it often had the opposite effect from what he wanted.

It was on February 14, 1941, at 12:13 pm, precisely by the Mickey Mouse clock on the commissary wall that Jerry and I entered the commissary, and I suddenly felt Jerry's hand with a vicelike grip invading my arm. He was staring at a table for four by the corner window and his jaw was moving up and down rapidly, as if he were chewing a particularly tough piece of leather, and he began to pant like a gorilla in heat. I wouldn't have been surprised if he had started banging his chest with his fists and bellowing loudly. But he only kept staring while little bubbles came flecking out of his mouth.

I followed his gaze and was immediately arrested by the most beautiful woman I had ever seen, striking me completely speechless as well. And remember, I was living in Los Angeles, where gorgeous blondes grew on the newly planted palm trees. She had hair of Pluto Yellow, penetrating eyes of Cinderella Blue, and the clear, bright complexion of Snow-White Peach/Beige with just a hint of Fawn

Brown freckles playing about the nose, typical of the American beauties from the Middle Western states, which was, it turned out, where she haled from. Her companion was a drab brunette of the mousey type, whose company she seemed to be enjoying thoroughly.

Jerry told me later, when I was in any condition to listen, that it felt like he was struck by a lightning rod and suddenly all those little birds that hovered around Snow White while she dressed had filled the cantina, and flowers were sprouting out of all the floors and walls.

"My god, what a dish! Quick," he said, "just grab anything and let's sit down with them before they leave or someone else takes those seats. Jeez, I can't imagine why they're sitting alone, unless it's because no one wants to get caught up with that plain little snip she's with."

Jerry, the born and bred New Yorker with plenty of girl experience and just enough moxie for a platoon of GIs, sat himself right down in front of her without so much as a "mind if we sit here?" and immediately launched into his routine.

"Hello there, gorgeous. Hope it's okay if we join you."

"Well, hello, handsome," she replied, for Jerry was indeed of the chiseled persuasion. "Don't be a wolf and we'll let you linger. I'm Margaret. You can call me Maggie. This is Alice. You can call her Alice."

"I'm Jared, but you can call me Jerry; and this continental charmer with me is David and you can call him Dave."

"What drags you dreamboats in here?"

"We work here," Jerry replied. "But I've never seen you here before."

"Well, that's because we've never been here before."

"So, what drags you dolls in here?"

"I'm on a day job. Singing. Alice, too."

"Who do you sing for?"

"Well, I suppose you could say I'll sing for anyone who'll pay me, but right now we are doing some of the songs for the new movie. About an elephant."

"*Dumbo!*" Jerry cried.

"Hey, who you calling 'dumbo'? I'll have you know I've been to college, you knucklehead!"

"Oh no! That's the name of the movie. '*Dumbo!*' He's an elephant. I'm working on it too. I think that brings us closer together, don't you?"

By this time, of course, Mousey and I were basically forgotten; it was all the Jerry-and-Maggie show.

"Gee Willikens, if you were any fresher, you'd still be on the hoof! What do *you* do here?" she asked.

"I'm an animator. So how long are you singing for?"

"Well, you could say I've been singing since I was three. I also act, and I was hoping to make it on Broadway. I did some back up work for Tex Beneke and Helen Forrest, but that was a dead end. So, then I thought I'd try the pix. That's why I came out here. I'm just doing session work to keep from falling through the sewer grate until I'm discovered. I'm here at Disney for just a couple of days… only three songs."

"Well, in that case," said Jerry, "will you marry me?"

"No thanks, Romeo," Maggie replied without a pause, blink or blush, "but I'd be glad of a free meal. Dinner instead? You can pitch woo over the cocktails."

"It's a date!" Jerry said enthusiastically.

"Hey, David called Dave, why not ask Alice called Alice to join us?"

The only one who brightened at this suggestion was Alice herself, but I guess I didn't mind tailing along just to see how this would turn out. I'd seen Jerry through a few brief romances already and this one promised to be intriguing.

When we returned to the work room, there was quite a storm stewing. The inbetweeners were hard at work but some of the more senior animators were getting quite animated. Jack Kinney, Fred Moore, Art Babbit and Al Zinnen were all surrounding Ben and giving him a good what-for.

"Walt's expecting too much too fast. We can't work under these conditions."

"He's stripping it all down."

"I don't mind the reduction in colors, but it's starting to look awfully flat."

"The whole pink elephants on parade is basically just sketches."

"Listen," Ben tried calming people down, "you wanted elephants in here to study how they move, and we did that, didn't we? That was a huge expense just so you could get the details right."

Everyone began shouting at once.

"Details? What a crock of shit!"

"More than a crock with that damn elephant…"

"C'mon, it's the least he could do…"

"Details! Oh c'mon! We're not doing faces on the roustabouts even, let alone the crowd!"

"It's all nothing but smearing…"

"And what's with the watercolors?"

"Look, we had to lay off a bunch of ink-and-paint girls. It's tough out there."

"I think it's time for union. We're the last studio holding out. I say, 'Union NOW!'"

Now, I may lean socialistic, but I was never much of a wobbly, and Jerry, like I said, even less, so we just kept our heads down and got to work.

Jerry's first date with Maggie was your basic "dinner and a movie", the dinner being at the Brown Derby, the movie being *The Devil and Miss Jones*. Over dinner, Jerry proposed early and often, and, while such assertiveness didn't seem to be terribly putting-off for his date, she also turned him down just as frequently as he proposed and tried to keep the conversation open, especially as Mousey and I had very little to say to one another, although I do believe she tried rather.

"Lookee here, Honeybun," she finally said after, I think, his twenty-third attempt, "I've heard all about you. One of the gals said you were a doll-dizzy lady-killer, making time with every floozy that came along, so you can bottle that lovey-dovey crapola, and let's just have a good time."

Jerry looked utterly shocked and tried to defend himself, but she cut him off.

"Turn it off, Dumbo. I mean, you're fine for cutting the rug or a night at the pix, but there's no way I'm marrying an inbetweener. You guys can't scratch two nickels together. In fact, I'm interested in seeing how you're gonna pay for dinner."

"I'm not just an inbetweener," Jerry cried, "I'm going to be big someday. Bigger than Picasso! Wait till I paint my masterpiece!"

"And you wait until I replace Ginger Rogers and Deanna Durbin!"

"I don't need to wait. I want you now."

"Keep wanting, ducky, but stop trying to make time. I'm looking for a sugar daddy, not a deadbeat Dumbo artist."

Mousey seemed to find that particularly funny, but it left Jerry rather flat, and talk was pretty muted for the rest of dinner. But the movie was quite good. We split afterwards as I took Mousey home.

"How can I make enough money to win her over?" he asked me later that night. "With all that work during the day, I don't have time to paint for myself, and until I hit it big, I'm up the creek without a paddle."

"Maybe just a pay rise will do. If we do go ahead with the union, that might turn the trick, don't you think?"

And just like that, we were with Art Babbitt, Willie Pyle, and Herb Sorrell, ready to walk out if we didn't get more pay.

And walk out we did, on May 29, in the middle of the day, and marched with signs and everything right in front of the Disney Studio main gate. The music was already completed by then so Maggie and Mousey had left, but Jerry kept in touch with her and kept dating. Money was especially tight during the strike, so dating for the two of them was severely constrained. I joined them a couple more times, which I think Maggie enjoyed as it tended to temper old Jerry's passionate outbursts. It was touching how much of those evenings she spent talking with me, even when Mousey joined as my date.

The strike did give Jerry time to finish a couple of large works, but if there was any interest in them, Jerry never found out where. By the time the strike settled in July, Jerry was in what I would call a depression despite our getting rather substantial pay increases. Right at that time, Maggie got a job as Swing for the B road company of *Pal Joey* and ended up on the road for months. Evidently, the night before she decamped for Dubuque, she and Jerry had a break-up fight.

"She hates me."

"I hardly think that could be true."

"No, she hates me. She said so. She said she wished she never saw my sour puss again. Those were her exact words. 'Sour puss.' What was the point of getting a raise if I can't have Maggie."

"We can get some nicer digs," I offered as consolation.

We did, but Jerry continued in his poignant fashion, hardly painting at all. It was so heavy around the flat, I almost called Mousey for a date. He wrote Maggie frequently but with no reply. He followed her schedule and finally flew out to meet her in Denver but came back even more depressed.

That December we had, you will, of course, remember, the "date which will live in infamy," and Jerry, after a rather heavy night of drinking, decided to enlist, and off he went to boot camp, leaving me with the full rent and Mousey's phone number. Fortunately, by then I got a promotion at Disney – now part of the background design team – and could afford it, and to be perfectly frank, Alice was starting to grow on me a bit. We had some fun times until she decided to move back to Peoria.

I kept in touch with Jerry, although the mail was a little unreliable most times and his heavily redacted letters told me little about his life, other than that it was fairly horrible. The constant wailing and gnashing of teeth over Maggie were the only sections left untouched by the censors, and they were, to be perfectly honest, pretty tedious.

Then, suddenly, she was back… and looking for Jerry! I informed her over the phone that he was now somewhere in Africa, or maybe Italy at that point. She demanded to see me and get all the "gory details." We met at Musso and Frank. I'd had another promotion by then and wanted to impress her.

"He said you gave him the raspberry, so he went off to fight for liberty and justice for all."

"The Big STIFF! Just because I called him cheesy, he goes and cheeses it! What a Dumbo he is!"

"So, you didn't give him the kiss-off?"

"Kiss-off? Jerry? My dreamboat?! C'mon! I love him like a ton of bricks. Did from the moment I saw him."

"It was love at first sight?"

"You bet your butter-colored knickers it was! Omigod! What if he never comes home? What'll I do?"

Afraid the waterworks were about to start, I mumbled some encouraging phrase or two before questioning her any farther.

"But you still wanted to wait until *you* made it big, right?"

"Made it big, right! Now *I'm* the Dumbo! Last audition I had they said 'Can't act. Can't dance. Can sing a little.' Jeesh! Yeah, that ship has left the station. I know, I thought I was the next sweater girl, and he thought he was the next Picasso, but I'm really just a second-rate canary and third-rate hoofer and you and I both know Jerry, God love him, wasn't meant for the Rive Gauche any more than I was meant for Broadway."

"You were meant for each other."

"You got that right, brother."

"So, what's the plan, ma'am?"

"I dunno, Dave. What if he doesn't come home? Or comes home with some French girl? God, Dave, I swear I'm so gone over him, I can't see straight."

"I can give you his APO address. You could write."

"I dunno. After what you said, do you really think I should write him?"

It wasn't rhetorical. She looked at me steadily, searchingly, making me feel like I was drowning. She really wanted a real answer, and I was torn in two about how to reply as she stared at me, with those pleading eyes. I was quite speechless for several moments with shock and fear. Finally, I gave the only answer I could:

"That's something you have to decide."

And so, she decided. And she wrote. And Jerry returned, making it from Omaha Beach to Berlin and back to Hollywood. I was now high up enough at "The Mouse" (as we began to call the company) to get him a decent job there, but he took advantage of the GI bill to get a degree and got a job in Phoenix working for a bank. Maggie and he married shortly before they moved there. I visited them regularly and was godfather to their firstborn, David Louis Mentnor. Two more followed, and they were, in a word, just the perfect family. Maggie got even lovelier in motherhood, and Jerry was, surprisingly, a wonderful father. So, in a sense, as a mother, Maggie did become a star. And good old Jerry, in a sense, created his masterpiece… his family.

I visited often at first, and they came out to LA once, but after that, it was really just letters and the rare long-distance phone call. It wasn't them. They were always truly thrilled to have me. No, it was me. The visits were always just a little bit too bittersweet for me.

For, you see, that fateful day in May 1941, that fateful moment but a few minutes past noon, in that commissary, Maggie and Jerry were not the only ones to fall in love at first sight. I did as well. And, no, not with Mousey, but with Maggie herself. It wasn't just her beauty nor her pure midwestern wholesomeness, nor her divine voice, nor the way she looked at you with those soft cerulean eyes as if you were the only person in the world that mattered. There was an aura of sanctity about her, a precious aspect that hung around her like a moonbeam, a mesmerizing, erotic, salubrious quality that stimulated you but also calmed you at the same time; like you were traveling through the universe at light speed, but at the same time, you were perfectly still, sitting quietly in a home you had made together. Which is precisely what Jerry did… with Maggie. While I, though moving ever upwards at work, remained, at home, a mere resident alien, quite alone, forever.

SOB

March 17, 2005

"Hey, Randy! Boss wants you. ASAP!"

"What?"

He could barely hear above the noise on the factory floor. His ever-efficient secretary knew from long experience that that was the loudest she could manage through the intercom and chose not to repeat herself. The operator of the tablet machine, situated as she was about midway between the intercom speaker and the plant manager, relayed the message. Randy concluded his now abbreviated discussion with the chief compounder and made for the door to ungown and head over to the main office.

He was the last to arrive, noting that all the other department heads were already there: R&D, IT, QC/QA, Accounting, Document Control, Customer Service, and Pam, the attractive Office Manager with whom he'd been trying to renew a moribund relationship for the past month. Frank Longwell, "the old man," was conspicuous by his absence, but the COO, his son, Sebastian, was sitting behind the old, mahogany roll-top desk. The room was silent, with tension one could almost smell. Sebastian rose as Randy entered.

"We're all here now. I'm not going to lead into this slowly because I don't really know how, so I'm just going to hit you with the bad news. Be prepared. You all know that my dad has suffered from IBD for a number of years. Yesterday, he was rushed to the ER with what seemed like a perforated bowel. When the doctors went in, they found considerably more damage than they reckoned and…" Sebastian continued, tearing up, "… well, not to drag this out… my father died on the operating table last night."

The effect was like an explosion combined with a kick in the stomach, with starts, gasps, cries, at least one scream, and the sudden movements of hands to open mouths. Sebastian was clearly having difficulty continuing to speak. Randy, initially staring into the middle distance, trying to absorb the awful news, glanced around at all the reactions, not the least that of Pam hugging the CFO, giving him a second reason for shock and loss.

The rest of the meeting was short and platitudinous. Some were still recovering from the blow, while others were already wondering about their future or the future of their departments. But this was neither the time nor the place for any questions of that kind. That didn't prevent side conversations, however, after Sebastian left to handle the details of his father's demise, comfort his family, and basically deal with the issue himself, but, absent any hard information, it was all speculation and emotion, with each person recalling the last time they spoke with the old man – for most, only a couple of days prior. Nothing really could be settled for some time, they knew.

Randall "Randy" Joseph, Plant Manager, and Nathan "Nate" Silverman, Director of R&D, the only managers who were also part-owners of Longwell Pharmaceutics, were acutely concerned, both because of their long association with the firm and their friendship with Frank, but mostly because, as shareholders, they had additional responsibilities and other priorities. They discussed between themselves the proper interval to wait before approaching Sebastian, but it was, in fact, he who took the initiative, calling them in for a meeting a mere ten days after the funeral.

"First, I want to thank you both for the flowers and the kind words. Nate, I know you knew my dad the longest of anyone here, and I really appreciate the words you spoke at his funeral. It was truly beautiful. I know my mom appreciated it, and I think she mentioned that to you."

"Yes, Sebastian, she did. Thank you."

"But with all that, I am sure you are wondering about the future, and, especially, the future of the LRP project."

The two veteran employees' attention immediately intensified, frozen on the young man who had taken the reins of the firm. LRP was Nate's baby, which he had been nursing for several years, a new chemical entity he developed and patented, although, as was common practice in the industry, he had signed the patent over to the company, but with a contract that entitled him – and Randy, who also contributed much to the project – to a royalty. The LRP project was going to revolutionize the company; LRP-0408, the latest iteration of the molecule, promised to be the most advanced and effective treatment to date for CKD. But funding an undertaking this massive was always going to be problematic for a firm as small as Longwell, and, as much as they admired and even loved the old man, their loyalty did not preclude their concern at his continued reluctance to invest in the project. Each man had significant, though different, issues with his son, but if Sebastian was going to move forward where Frank had hung back, they were perfectly at ease in shifting their loyalty from the kindly, yet obdurate, old fuddy to his callous, yet more venturesome, son.

"As you both know, getting an NDA for an NCE is a pretty expensive proposition. The IQ, OQ, and PQ on the compounding equipment alone are over a quarter mil, and that's before we get to the clinicals, which would be in the tens of millions.

"Well, I am happy to say that we will have funding to proceed with hiring a CRO and to proceed with the clinicals and on through full NDA apps. But it comes at a cost. As you know, there was no way we could go it alone, or I should say, go it without a loan. But my father was always risk-averse when it came to taking on debt, as you know. As for bringing in the VCs, or even just one larger partner, he was just as afraid to cede any control like that. It was I who invited Novo-LillVie in for discussions, but my dad just couldn't see his way to going down that road. I, on the other hand, am now prepared to take those necessary steps to get LRP done.

"Phil Glassman, the VP of BD at NLV, whom you've both met, will be flying out here tomorrow to discuss the details of a JV. You know that we've had a CDA in place on this for a while and even got to an MOA, although we were unable to agree on a term sheet because of my dad. I'm not saying I am prepared to meet those exact terms now, but I think the deal they proposed had promise, and I am at least willing to take that as a starting point for further discussions. Of course, nothing will be decided or signed without your approvals. In addition to your positions here at LPI – not to mention your close connection with my mom and sister and so on – you are, after all, shareholders. I know you both appreciate what my father did for you when I first joined the company, and I hope you know that I would never take a step that you both didn't approve of. And since you are both on board for royalties from LRP, I know you will be happy that the project is moving forward, and PDQ at that."

If the death of the old man was a shock to Nate and Randy, the news that the deal with one of the largest members of the Big Pharma club was back on the table was paralyzing, at least to their vocal cords. Both had, indeed, met with Phil Glassman, and both had had the same reaction as Sebatian's father – a sense of looking into a deep, black pit. The old man said it would be like "dancing with the devil" to get into bed with NLV, the thought of which made even them somewhat nervous. But they also knew that the LRP project was a potential blockbuster drug that would catapult Longwell Pharma into the stratosphere, if not ionosphere, of the pharmaceutical world with the potential of making it an international presence, while also, incidentally, making them, with promised royalties, fabulously rich.

The news spread through the office, factory, and warehouse like a whirlwind, with everyone expressing a strained optimism. Life at LPI was pretty good if one did their job, kept their head down, and accepted the thousands of decisions, ructions, and modifications of rules and procedures endemic to their industry. Only an FDA inspection caused any palpable alarm or concern. But the news of a joint venture with a huge pharma company meant that life would change for all two hundred plus employees, and they knew it. One could, at this point, only hope it would be for the better.

*****

"If the old bastard hadn't given those two assholes shares when I came on board it would be smooth sailing," Sebastian confessed to Jim Nugent, his fellow SOB, that evening at their bi-monthly meeting. "He thought it would smooth things over. Like he owed those fucking idiots anything. What a crock! They've been a pain in the ass for years, having to treat them like equals and shit. But with the sale of the company, it's going to be really difficult getting them to sign off without giving away the whole shootin' match."

"I thought you said it was a JV. The company'd be equal partners with Novo-LillVie, no?"

"Who could be equal partners with that fucking monster? *And* it would take me years to get my money out. No, I'm going for a sale. I'll let Nate and Randy know only after the deal is done. But the real problem is..."

At that point, Sebatian was interrupted by the arrival at his table of the President of the SOBs. "Sons Of the Boss" was started back in the 1960s as a purely social group by a handful of young men who had the questionable privilege of working for their fathers. Jim had put Sebastian up for membership the week he joined Longwell Pharma, after his disastrous stint at the consulting firm that hired him right out of college. For years, he had enjoyed the meetings, not just for the social aspect, but for the networking opportunities and helpful discussion sessions as well.

"Sorry to interrupt, gentlemen, but I have to discuss something rather unpleasant with Sebastian here. Look, Seb, you've been a good member in good standing of the SOBs for a number of years now, and you've contributed much to our lively discussions, but – and I am sorry for your loss – but the fact is that you're now the boss since your father passed away, and therefore no longer eligible as a member of this club. Remember, we're Sons of the Boss, not the Bosses of Sons."

"Aw, Richard, come on, don't be an asshole. You're not taking the club name literally. I mean, you started letting women in 10 years ago and kept the name 'sons'."

"True, but they are all working for their dads or moms, and, let's face it, the name is more clever than COB, Children of the Boss. Our purpose is to provide guidance and support for that unique and difficult relationship of a child working for their parent. And it's been helpful to us all, as it has been for you too, I think. You can't say we haven't been helpful."

"Shit, Richard, of course you have. That's why I want to stay in."

"But you don't *need* our help anymore, Seb. You *are* the boss, so that dynamic is over for you. You know you can't stay. It's SOP. Remember when Marc Levin had to leave. Same reason. Them's the rules."

"So, you're kicking me out because my dad died…"

"Think of it as graduating. You didn't stick around your old college after you graduated, did you? No, you went out into the world and made a name for yourself. Time for you to go out into the world and be your own boss."

"OK, asshole. I'll leave."

"Oh no, Seb, you're fine for tonight. Stick around. Have another drink. And I know you and Jim were close, and, of course, I'm sure you will continue to meet on your own. Have a nice night, both of you!"

"Asshole," Sebastian repeated after the SOB president left.

"Always has been," his companion commented, draining his glass and calling for another.

*****

Throughout the negotiations with Novo-LillVie, Sebastian provided regular updates to the company's management team and the Board, always referring to the deal as a joint venture even as he worked to sell the company outright. Of course, his mother and sister knew from the beginning, each expressing some concern for what the final solution would entail, but both willing to let Sebastian lead the way. Nate and Randy only learned once the deal was fully formulated, and he needed to get Board approval.

They expressed certain misgivings, but on learning that they would each receive an immediate payment in excess of half a million and would receive a 5% royalty each on all net sales of LRP, once approved and on the market, they assented with pleasure. It helped as well that the entire management team would get employment contracts, of varying lengths, theirs being the most substantial, with a 5-year term and two automatic renewals with raises upon the mutual consent of both parties. They even found meeting with Phil Glassman, as they had to do several times during due diligence, less unpleasant over time and, when he handed them, at closing, each their check – which turned out to be over $100,000 more than expected – he seemed positively charming.

After nearly two years post-close, however, very little was proceeding on the LRP project, and nothing new was coming out of R&D, which, along with Finance, had been transferred to the Novo-LillVie HQ in New Jersey. Randy expressed concern that production seemed to be slowing while Nate was more than a little bothered that all work necessary to get approval of the drug was delayed while they ran only one small, open-label study.

"It's a dose-ranging study," Phil explained. "Before we commit to a multi-site, double-blind, placebo-controlled clinical, with all races, ages, ethnicities, and genders listed fully and properly in the inclusion criteria, we need to zero in on a proper dosage."

It was a reasonable position and, as Nate accepted it, so did Randy, whose attention anyway was focused now on Pam, who, after the deal closed, found Randy far more interesting again, especially after the CFO was let go. Their relationship blossomed over the next several years, even as the LRP project seemed to lie fallow and production schedules languished.

*****

Sebastian stared out at the ocean, his sweating Mai-Tai in hand, nearly finished, his lovely wife, Diane, by his side, with her own drink in one hand and her phone in the other, prattling merrily while watching their two adorable children playing in the sand. She was quite pleased to have secured this quiet place in Maui for the month, only disappointed by the fact that Wailea beaches were all public, so that, occasionally, someone wandered by to disturb their solitude. Sebastian was content to let his mind drift after deciding where they would dine that night and exactly which brand of scotch he would order for his cocktail.

He and Novo-LillVie had mutually decided not to renew his contract after the five years, settling on a mere consulting agreement with much less to do and with a significant pay cut. But that didn't matter to Sebastian, as he had already received the last of his $10 million milestone payments, compared to which his $1 million a year salary was but a drop in the bucket. The contract was critical, however, providing him the excuse to travel when and where he wanted, most frequently to Chicago or New York, where each of his mistresses was in residence.

It had taken him some time to restructure the company, splitting it into a web of interlocking, albeit legally separate, entities, relegating the lesser assets to companies with the original partners and the greater asset of the LRP formulation to a company entirely his own. Of course, he made sure his mother and sister were adequately taken care of. It had taken slightly more finesse to calculate the exact amount of downstroke necessary to keep Nate and Randy happy and unconcerned with the deal's details. Providing them an additional $125,000 at closing, he knew, would seal their oblivious attitude, at least long enough for him to move most of his assets offshore, where even Diane knew not where. If they were ever to divorce – that would be after the children were much older – he knew she would be fine with the house in Sausalito and a million or so in the bank to keep her perfectly satisfied.

As for the royalty payments, he had no part in those, and it was irrelevant anyway, as LRP would never come to market. As Phil Glassman had explained to him the very first day, "NLV has already developed a similar NCE, close enough to LRP that there could be patent infringement. We're not really buying Longwell so much as the LRP patent, which we'll designate as 'prior art' and then we can move forward with our own product without any infringement issues. Also, initial tests indicate that LRP could be a cure, while our NCE is still a treatment. That means the patient will be on it for life. We generally prefer that kind of drug to a one-and-done, for obvious reasons. Our R&D team also has a strong aversion to NIH assets in general, but with that ridiculous 10% royalty, this was a no-brainer for everyone at NLV."

The math was obvious. If the LRP drug did what they had forecasted, that royalty would have cost NLV nearly $100 million a year. With Sebastian eager to sell, they could avoid the royalty by procuring the asset for slightly more than just one year's royalty payment.

"So, you're buying LRP just to bury it?" Sebastian had asked.

"It'll be DOA the minute we ink the deal," Phil replied candidly.

"But what about the manufacturing plant and the other products. We're a generics company. You want to get into the generic drug business?"

"No, of course not. We'll sell off the ANDAs and shutter the plant in five to ten years. Anything we want to keep, we'll validate in Parsippany and finish the tech transfer before your contract is up."

The mumblings about the perfect timing of his father's death for Sebastian to effectuate this deal, and the inevitable rumors that swirled as a result, engendered a passing discomfort, but he was confident, especially after all this time – not to mention the complete lack of evidence – that nothing from that quarter was going to disturb his Utopian life.

The children frolicked in the sand, stomping on the castles they had just made, darting into the waves from time to time, screaming with laughter while they were battered about by the salted foam, all as the sun drew lower in the sky. He and Diane always enjoyed this part of the day. After the glorious sunset, the children would be ushered up to the condo and showered by the nanny. He and Diane would dine out, perhaps with another couple, and return to an early bedtime. Their month in Maui was almost up and Sebastian was already pleasantly anticipating the return home and, shortly after that, his heading to Biarritz alone where he would meet up with one of his two lovely ladies in waiting.

He still regretted losing his membership in Sons of the Boss, but drew a quaintly perverse satisfaction that, in nearly every other aspect of his life, he remained a superb, even perfect, SOB.

Me Too

August 10, 2017

Sitting at the hi-top by the window in the bistro, he was able to see, without being seen, the full length of the street from which she would most likely approach the door. The freezing blast of air conditioning, seemingly from just on top of him, mixed with the light suit of sweat he had donned during the brief walk from his car, inducing, at least initially, a mild shiver from time to time.

The young waitress had deposited the menu and asked for his drink order. He had demurred, preferring to wait for his guest. The menu now sat in front of him, still unopened, as he gazed blandly into the outer world. Cars crawled by, but he wasn't really looking at cars as he had no idea what kind of car she drove these days. He was looking at pedestrians, if they seemed at all to be approaching the restaurant's door.

He almost missed it. It was sudden, after all. Despite the vibrant, flowery summer dress – an unusual choice considering where she worked – there was no mistaking her, as the unexpected pinch of fear in his gut worked its way rapidly to his suddenly clouded brain. He had decided to be staring nonchalantly at his menu as she approached the table so he could appear to be surprised by her arrival, but as she disappeared from view while entering the restaurant he found that he could not help but steal covert glances toward the front door, allowing their eyes to connect as she entered the room, ruining his plan.

Rising, with just a hint of confusion as she approached, he wondered if a sartorial comment was appropriate, determining almost immediately that it would not be. She, smiling brightly, walking confidently, flicking her hair back with the hand not grappling the substantial handbag, gave him a quick, though hardly perfunctory, hug, as she was always wont to do – and not just with him – before mouthing a trifling pleasantry and mounting the bistro seat with ease and grace. He, too, having risen to meet and be hugged, found his seat and tried to match the brilliance, without the depth, of her smile, but almost immediately reverted to a neutral expression, fearing his bright smile could be perceived as a lascivious grin.

"Wow," she said, "You haven't changed a bit!"

"Oh well," he said, with a mild simper as he mentally calculated whether the time they'd been apart warranted such a comment. "Maybe a few gray hairs, a few wrinkles, a couple pounds. You, however, haven't changed a bit. Still glorious you!"

She gave the compliment all the attention it deserved as he registered the regrettable mishit. Avoiding any reference to her new look – the colorful flowing dress, the longer hair with lighter highlights and its slightly more vivid floral scent, the sharp red gash that replaced the subtle pink lips of her former mouth, and the eyes with just a touch more mascara and shadow – he tried a reboot.

"I'm so happy to see you!"

"Me too! I was so pleasantly surprised by your email."

"I know! I was thinking about you the other day, and it occurred to me that it's been too long, you know, so that's when I… I mean, we were… well, we did… you know… all those projects and sales calls and… It just seemed to me…"

As he foundered, she found the rest of the sentence for him, effortlessly piloting the conversation to people and events of their shared time and, after a time, instituting a deft segue to a more recent vintage while he was tacking as best he could through the snarled thicket of her running commentary.

He had forgotten how much she talked, how much he enjoyed their chats, and how pleasant he found her voice, even as he worked to glean her meaning from its timbre, alternating nervous glimpses of her face with truculent glares at the smooth, hard surface of the large, dark, wood, octagonal hi-top. She'd always complained of the office being cold. He wondered if she was now finding the restaurant, as he was, rather on the frigid side.

She really had been surprised. But pleasantly so, she wanted to be certain he knew. When some people move on, they really move on, she had said to Carolyn when his absence reached several months. But some people are like that. She understood. Never look back. She got that. Would she be like that? She could not see not seeing Carolyn or Jessica if she left. She knew he hadn't contacted anyone else, not even Ira, so, yes, she was telling the absolute honest truth that that email was a surprise, and a pleasant one at that. He was glad to hear it. She was glad that he chose this restaurant.

"Yeah, I always liked this place."

"Me too."

The well-tatted, nose-ringed slip of a waitress floated over and, with blackened lips, informed them that her name was Sheila and that she would be taking care of them. This now firmly established, Sheila inquired what each would like to drink. He had his usual iced tea; she evidently had not changed from her customary Diet Sprite. And, unsurprisingly, she did indeed ask if the A/C could be turned down. Sheila acknowledged the request without actually promising anything, despite her earlier promise that she would be taking care of them, as she left to put in the drink order, leaving cold uncertainty in her wake.

The time he'd spent worrying what to do if the conversation lagged could have been employed in happier and more productive pursuits. The beverage order given and taken, she launched into a series of questions about his new position that, in less time than it took for her to glance at the menu, went from catching up to what was beginning to feel a bit like an interrogation. Still, it was safe terrain. He was happy to let the conversation flow this way, filling her in on his new office environment, giving wisplike impressions of people in a flurry of names, titles, and positions, tied only to nebulous expressions of who was on his team and who was very much not. Noting that she avoided anything tied to life outside of work, he also gave those subjects a wide berth, as he asked her about old colleagues, where everyone in the old department stood these days, who was up, and who down, finishing, understandably, with who replaced him.

"Oh, I get along with Aaron just fine. I mean, he's not you, of course. And Anne feels the same, I know, so it's not just me."

"Well, that's very kind of both of you."

"I'm not trying to suck up to you, you know!" she said with a laugh. "I mean, what's the point, you're not my boss anymore, right?"

"Yes, that's true," he responded, trying to keep his voice as light as hers.

"Not that you couldn't be again, I suppose."

Feeling slightly tremulous at not quite knowing where all this was going, he kept his eyes steady but tried not to look directly at her for too long while also trying not to obviously avoid looking, especially when she laughed at her "suck up" comment, to which he had timidly joined. He was delighted, therefore, when Sheila returned with their drinks and deadpanned that she was ready to take their order, which she then, taking care of them now as she had promised them before, proceeded to do. His order took two seconds, while hers was complicated somewhat by the various items held, added, or on the side.

Neither one quite knew how to begin again after the order-taking. He was trying to decode her comment about working for him again, feeling that it was, at least on its surface, a good sign but also, very possibly, a veiled threat. He did not realize how long he was quietly perseverating until she interrupted his thoughts.

"Do you regret it?"

"What?"

"Leaving."

He seemed to hesitate just a sliver of a moment.

"No. Not really. I mean, I miss everyone, you know, but I think it's been good for me. The job is challenging – it's a larger team, you know – so in a good way. I've met some great people, like I said, and we've done some really creative work, too. More responsibility, of course, but also more freedom, you know. Learned a lot, too."

"Sounds like you're happy there."

"Yes, I'm happy, I guess. You? Still?"

"Oh yes me too still I suppose. Not that I wouldn't be open to something new if it came along."

"Oh, sure. I guess that's how I felt when the job at Newman came up."

"So, tell me more about this wonderful new place. It sounds really fascinating. Like, what are you working on now?"

He knew he had to be vague, talking mostly about process and structure, adding to her one-word vocabulary of "department" such enticing offerings as "team," "sub-committee," "working group," and "squad" and how each intersectionalized with the other, the overlapping goals, the splitting of work, sharing of clients, the focus groups, remote meetings, and light travel. He dazzled her with voluptuous new terms like "Growth Hacking," "Big Data," and "Micro Moments." An avalanche of acronyms poured from his nervous lips, and soon, she was swimming in SEOs, KPIs, ABMs, and POVs. The restaurant was starting to warm as he warmed to his subject.

"Sounds like a pretty full crew. Still, it's a much larger place. I assume people come and go all the time. Has anyone started since you started? Do you do any hiring? I mean, I was just wondering what that looked like you know when you're looking for someone. Has that come up yet?"

"Not really."

"Oh, come on you're holding out," she smiled with another playful flip of the hair. "I mean, you've been there quite a while now. Are you telling me that you haven't yet fired someone, or someone left or that a position opened up and you haven't had to hire anyone? No? Really? I was just wondering, no big deal, you know. It's not like I'm looking, you know. I'm still happy there. I mean it's comfortable, you know. I've made lots of friends, and I know the environment, too."

"Well, you've been there quite a while."

"I know! Like, it's been ten years, right? I mean, like, I came right out of college. Who would've thought!"

Neither one had expected her to stay so long at the same job. Of course, she had had a couple of promotions, so that tends to keep one in place, but she was a little disappointed that she hadn't been tapped for his position when he left, and there was another promotion that came up afterwards that she was passed over for too. That was frustrating, to say the least. Of course, he hadn't expected to be there that long himself, he had to admit. Still, people were shocked when he left for the white-shoe, downtown firm. Were they really? Oh yes, there were several mixed comments, tinged with not a little concern that he might skim off the cream where he had been. He knew that might be the case, which is why he'd been careful, circumspect, and quaintly silent to all that he had left behind, clients and colleagues alike. Until now.

"Yes, until now."

"To see me!"

Lost in a desperate search for a subtext in that throwaway, he reflected that it wasn't really out of line, given its self-obvious truth, so he decided not to read too much into it, even as he kept trying to divine the nuances of her comments. He had been floundering in a shabby attempt to drag the conversation from the present back to the past, and now that he had, he wasn't sure how to introduce his all-important topic. His pause must have been longer than he grasped as she chose once again to jump in to fill the awkward silence.

"Yeah, I guess I assumed you would have reached out to Ira or Bruce first, but I'm quite complimented that it was me. Of course, you and I worked closely on a number of accounts. In fact, there was talk around the office that you kind of favored me."

He forced his eyes to meet hers as his insides melted like spring snow on a warm afternoon, sapping what feeble resolve he'd had, circling the drain of terror. Her trenchant mien gave no indication of a hidden message as she once again flipped her hair over her ear, tossing again that captivating, ineffable essence into the atmosphere between them, but in place of the usual open, dazzling smile, she proffered an admittedly more professional and appropriate, though frighteningly ambiguous, deadpan that cut straight through him.

Praying he betrayed no emotion, he looked around for inspiration. The plastic tables outside by the sidewalk, covered in pale blue flower-printed plastic tablecloths, surrounded by white plastic chairs, devoid of customers on this sweltering day, provided no answer. Indoors, the black and white checkered floor gliding by the insipid artwork, and the long, oak bar under the copper enameled ceiling, and the slow winding fans distributing the now tepid air, ruffling napkins, and the faux flowers on various tables also offered no advice. He was about to fill the electrically charged moment with a vapid banality when she saved him by continuing.

"Oh yes it's true. Look, you're gone now so you can admit it. Everyone thought you like favored me I know they did and yes we agreed a lot and we worked together probably more than like maybe you did with the others, but I know it was because you like respected me and my work product not for any other reason, right?"

And there it was. It came over the net so fast he thought for all the world she'd aced him. And yet, after a tortuous beat or two, there it still was, no follow-up, floating at eye level in the riot of her silence, then settling in the middle of the table, between the Sprite and iced tea, like a plate of sweetbreads, prepared to perfection, but a dish no one wants to touch. The moment had come to confront that terrible incident from their past; he thought he was prepared for it but found he was not, fumbling for words again, when he was saved by Sheila's arrival with the salad and his burger and fries. In the bustle of the food, he made the decision not to respond or acknowledge her challenge, but to come from a completely different direction, with the merest suggestion of an impression of that dreadful moment long past, hoping she would make a more explicit reference to it so he could deal with it once and for all.

"I really enjoyed those times. With you… and Carolyn and… Ira, and so on. I mean, I like my team now – don't get me wrong – and I think I've settled into the new culture well, you know, but, well… I really did enjoy our time together…"

"Oh, me too!"

"The whole department, of course, like I said, Carolyn and Jessica and so forth, but I do think you're right that you and I did most of the work. At least the creative side of it. Don't get me wrong, everyone contributed – no question about that – but, if you broke it down, I think you'll see that you and I were responsible for 80% of the deliverables. Or more. Really! It was always just you and me. And I was good with that. You were great, and I enjoyed it. The work, you know. It meant… something."

That was his best shot. Surely, she would respond to that, and then, one way or another, he'd know. But no, it was left hanging in the balance as she busied herself with her salad. Was she filling in time or was measuring the dressing really such a meticulous endeavor? He couldn't remember her doing that in lunches past.

He'd sold enough marketing plans to know when the client was weighing. And that it was time to be silent. But for how long? He looked up to see her looking down, carefully stabbing each leaf, cuke, scallion, and Garbanzo bean, and he knew enough time had gone by and it was time to bring this puppy into port.

"At least it meant something to me."

She looked up. Beguiled yet again, he was falling dizzy into those riveting blue eyes and the dense, black fear of what she might say next. As much as he needed her to bring the incident up, he still feared it. But again, she said, "Me too," with again a sultry hand through the hair, wrapping it around her ear, stirring him enough to require another bite of the burger, giving her time to follow up, but instead, she was off on another tangent. She remembered Carolyn doing more than he said. He accepted that she may be right about Carolyn and maybe Ira and, yes, okay, maybe Jessica too, but not about Anne or Linda or Bruce. Oh god, certainly not Bruce. They agreed on that!

"Oh, but you don't know about Bruce and Jessica. Well, it seems that he said something inappropriate to her – she didn't share – but it became like a big deal, and he got reassigned. But then, right after, I had this issue with Bill Proctor."

"From Boston General?"

"Yes, well, you know that was our account, and we used to call on him together but now it was mine and he, well, he started getting a little demonstrative, if I can put it that way, and finally he made like a move that was just, well, was frankly like pure harassment, like not subtle at *all,* and I wasn't sure quite what to do, so I reported it like you're supposed to and Aaron – I will say this for him, I think he handled it well considering he's like a client but he just reassigned Ira to the account and gave me NYCPC, which is actually like a bigger account so that kinda like worked out okay for me. I mean, I think I did the right thing reporting it, don't you?"

She had stopped talking. She had asked a question. His mind whirled, trying to figure out if this was a deliberate declaration, whether to respond or to ignore it, or to seize the moment and bring the past up explicitly himself. He'd come with a question to be answered, a question he could not ask but to which he needed an answer, and this was his opportunity – perhaps the only one he'd have at this point – but he had not had time to figure out how to phrase it within the context of this new revelation. He'd wanted to steer into port but not crash the dock.

"Well, considering it worked out well for you, I suppose it was the right thing to do."

"Yes, I suppose so," she said, with a laugh, throwing her rich tresses back again with her delicately manicured hand. She'd always been partial to French manicures, something he rather liked, both professionally and personally. Her sumptuous hair pulled back briefly by this action, he noted the roots were rather dark, indicating her last trip to the hairdresser must have been longer ago than to the nail salon.

"Still, it seems wrong that Bill got away with it. I mean, I'm happy with NYCPC – it's like really great, and I've had some great meetings with them – and their ad budget is like, what, double maybe so okay, in the end, but when you consider what Anne is dealing with..."

A frisson of anguish overwhelmed him as he tried frantically to glean understanding from the web of words spiraling past him, as he fell again into the deep well of that smile, the lush curve of her breasts, the barest hint of cleavage when she leaned forward, and the delicious way her fingers fidgeted with her fork and napkin. But this falling into old habits was counterproductive to his original intent for the lunch, and he tried to refocus. He had the impression, at this point, that they really did turn the air conditioning off just to please her. Or perhaps it was just the place filling up. At any rate, it was definitely warmer, noisier, and harder to hear. Continuing her flow as he fumbled with his food and thoughts, she now seemed to have returned to the issue of lost promotions.

"I think if I'm passed over again, I'll leave. It's just jealousy, you know. Because you were so good to me. It's your fault I'm stuck, I guess, so maybe you should offer me something."

Her immoderate laugh did nothing to alleviate his concern, his frozen smile the only indication of what was happening to his insides. This was certainly close to a threat. If only he could know for certain where it was coming from. He knew he had to tread carefully, but this was his moment to determine if she was thinking of another moment years ago. She did not bring up Bill Proctor again, and he was too afraid to try to do so himself. He had no place to put her, and he wouldn't hire her even if he did, unless he absolutely had to, so he had no direct answer to her probing question. He mumbled something unintelligible, hoping she didn't ask him to repeat it. Each felt their moment had passed as another pause settled in while he grappled with his hamburger and she with her salad.

She looked around. The restaurant seemed full of couples whose relationship was ambiguous, even with careful scrutiny. Work friends or just friends; tête-á-têtes, open or furtive; some were laughing and some frowning. The table of five in the corner, all men, was obviously a working group, even before they pulled out their pads and laptops. But then there was the table with three women, probably in their mid-sixties, maybe older, probably just come from the club or gym, they had that Lululemon look, even if the clothes were almost certainly knockoffs. She wondered what kind of working life they had before becoming just another gaggle of suburban jetsam, or if they'd had any at all, being of an age when women often went directly from school to kitchen. Or bedroom.

He seemed more intent on dealing with the juices seeping from his hamburger, the bottom bun now sodden, dilapidated, and useless, wiping the greasy residue from his hands with his napkin. She let the pause lie as well, quietly sneaking a few French fries from his plate. He liked that she didn't ask. He'd always liked that about her. It was, after all, her inferred intimacy that had invited his own back then, a move he relished at the time, despite her polite but firm putdown that followed. At last, she spoke again – delicate subjects left behind – and the conversation drifted as the meal drifted toward its tender coda. They covered weather, family, vacations, cruising, baseball, tennis, recent films, favorite TV shows, and other odd topics in a flurry of afterthoughts and final bites.

And just like that, a whole hour – no, more, an hour and a half – was gone, as he called for the check. She agreed that the time certainly seemed to pass quickly.

"I enjoyed every minute of it!"

"Me too!"

"Just like old times."

"Just like old times."

The check came quickly, the artless Sheila plopping it unceremoniously in the middle of the table.

"It's mine."

"Can we at least split it?"

"I asked you. That's the rule."

"No, the rule was that we went back and forth."

There seemed to be some talk about repeating. They agreed it would be nice, while he silently hoped it would never be necessary. He took the check with firm fingers and a weak smile. She acquiesced with a smile that overwhelmed the artificial lighting like an August sun.

With Sheila paid and well-tipped, they headed out, he eschewing the men's room, despite the long ride back to the office, hoping a vanishing hope that business might yet result in the brief walk to their cars. When he opened the restaurant door, they both felt and commented on the wall of heat. Like the door of a blast furnace opening, they agreed.

Their cars were in the same direction. They discussed whose court the ball was in, beginning the parting ritual as they sauntered down the sun-washed street, raising their voices above the traffic. The exact placement of the ball was unresolved. There was no opportunity now for anything other than platitudes. Moving her substantial handbag to the outer shoulder, her hand seemed to brush his gently as a result. As broiling as the afternoon was, it seemed to him even hotter.

At his car, she thanked him again, said she was looking forward to another lunch, and gave him another one of her signature hugs, lingering, it seemed to him, somewhat longer this time. He certainly was much more conscious of the fullness of her breasts as well as the dubious pleasure of their continued pressure against his chest. Lobbing caution gently into the air, he kept the hug a bit more than advisable, perhaps for the mild titillation, but more as if she were a shipwrecked piece of flotsam to which he clung to keep himself from drowning, a fragment of safety in a turbulent sea. But not only did it fail to provide even the glancing thrill he hoped for, it only emphasized the miserable lack of assurance he had been seeking. Certainly, more than ever, as they broke the clinch, he saw himself a slattern of fortune.

She tripped blithely down the street to her car with no look back to wave or smile. He heedlessly noted the shape of her legs, remembering them, with a little guilt, when more of them had been revealed, in time past, from skirts with higher hems. Standing on the curb, his hand seemingly glued to the car door handle, he felt weary and abused, knowing that his task was unfinished and fearing it may even have been undone, or perhaps as inappropriate in its conception as it was unresolved in its conclusion, while desperately hoping that it actually might have been completely unnecessary.

Shivering slightly despite the heat, as he watched her breeze quickly into her car, he reflected ruefully on what might have happened, all those years ago, had he not taken the hint and desisted, but instead had blazed forth regardless of the consequences even now knowing how vicious those consequences could be, especially now, and especially considering the enigmatic reassignment of Bruce, let alone to potential fallout of the Bill Proctor incident. Still, he could not help but think, despite his most explicit efforts, while standing outside his car, watching her apply the curious red lipstick while she peered at herself in her rear-view mirror, that things would certainly have turned out different, all those years ago, when she had been so tantalizing, and he had been so presumptuous, had they each, at the time, not been married.

A Painful Case

March 1, 1877

John Moulton came from a family long committed to the abolitionist movement. It was, therefore, perfectly natural that, when President Lincoln called for volunteers, he was eager to join the fight as quickly as possible. His father, the distinguished jurist Nathaniel Moulton, however, though equally committed to the sacred cause, expressed a strong wish that John complete his studies at Harvard first, as his older brother, Nathaniel Jr, had done the year prior. John, though disappointed, agreed and, applying himself assiduously, received his diploma at the end of First Term that year, joining the 15th Massachusetts Infantry only a few months after their disastrous engagement at Balls' Bluff. His brother had joined the 20th Infantry at the outset of the war.

Nathaniel Sr. used what influence he had to gain John a direct commission as First Lieutenant, as he had the elder brother, but John's lack of military experience limited his options to a lower rank. John served with distinction at the Siege of Yorktown, the Battle of Fair Oaks, and The Seven Days Battles, where the combination of the regiment's heavy losses and his own battlefield acumen earned him a brace of promotions. He acquitted himself well as Captain at the Second Battle of Bull Run but took a ball at Antietam.

It was touch and go whether or not he would keep his leg, the "butcher" more than once threatening the saw. But John insisted that he remain intact, regardless of the consequences. By the grace of God, he pulled through and was sent home with several medals, a distinct limp, and a constant ache, especially when walking. As painful as this was for him and his father, far worse was the distress of losing Nathaniel Jr. in the same battle.

John spent the remainder of the war at home, apprenticing with his father, with a short stint at a larger law office in Boston, a partner there being a close friend of the elder Moulton. Father and son practiced general law together until Nathaniel's untimely death in 1869.

John married his hometown sweetheart, Sarah Rossiter, shortly after his return to Storm River. The Rossiters, like the Moultons, were a distinguished family in the town, and Franklin and Hannah Rossiter were, like Nathaniel, very much in favor of the match. With a gimpy leg, the discomfort of which vexed him daily and severely constrained his activities, John felt that he had limited matrimonial opportunities, and as his childhood fondness for Sarah grew rapidly during his recuperation, he agreed to the marriage the parents had arranged. In addition to the agonizing leg wound, John also returned from war with a displaced freed slave, Vesta, who had agreed to act as housekeeper for his father and then, shortly after his wedding, for Sarah and himself.

The Moultons had a son rather quickly, but three years later, when Sarah's second pregnancy ran into difficulties – the child no longer being quick in the womb – mother and baby girl did not survive. John's torment at the loss reached an extent that surprised even his in-laws, who, John being newly orphaned as well, did their best to comfort him before they themselves resettled in one of the newer western states. Vesta, practically part of the family by that time, helped look after their young son, Caspar, while John labored through the agony of his loss.

John's law practice was firmly established at this point, so the time he had to take off to adjust to his new situation was clearly understood through the town. It helped, of course, that his father's good friend, Benjamin Baker, was mayor and had influence in helping him to retain his clients.

But Sarah's death was a sore that would not heal. The endless, excruciating heartache seemed to disburse to his wounded leg, requiring Doc Farlington to increase his laudanum dosage more than once. Adding to his burdens, young Caspar was becoming more unruly each day, and John, having lost his parenting partner, allowed his condition to alienate him from his delicate son, essentially leaving his upbringing entirely to Vesta. At the time our story opens, the boy had effectively abandoned schoolwork, roaming the town and surrounding woods with whatever other juveniles he could convince to join in his delinquency. As much as the Moulton family had been lauded in Storm River – and as much as John himself was held in high esteem, if only for his service to his country and his family's sacrifices – so was Caspar disrespected, other parents instructing their children to avoid the youngest Moulton.

"You need to do sumfin 'bout that boy o' yor'n," Vesta warned; "he gonna turn out a hoodoo man if'n you don't!"

"What can I do," replied John equably, "that you aren't already doing?"

"Stop sparin' the rod!" Vesta cried.

"I will not institute corporal punishment in my home," was John's firm reply.

"I ain't studyin' none o' that," the frustrated Vesta huffed. "Don't know nuffin 'bout no institutes nor corp'rals neither, but if that boy i'n't punished for his shenanigans, he fin t' end up no good to no body."

The good Vesta well knew the difference between a spanking and a whupping, having seen plenty of both in her life, and, as such, did not place all physical punishments under one rubric, as John did. The boy was a sheer rapscallion who needed strict discipline, and, for Vesta, discipline meant a switch – if certainly not the cat – as an instructor. Lessons, she knew from hard experience, are learned best when delivered with a sting.

But John seemed to have lost all interest in his son's upbringing which was left, to her dismay, for the reliable Vesta to attend to, doing her best under his strictures against physical chastisement. Vesta assumed John had seen enough in the war that he was just plain dead set against it, or possibly that, being in constant pain himself, he could not tolerate watching others endure any such hardship.

John was the only attorney in town and, loner as he'd become in widowerhood, so too had he no partner in the practice. Although he specialized in wills and trusts, John was, like his father, a generalist, handling a wide range of cases. In addition to drafting property deeds and the like, he advised on family matters, helped settle disputes, and, when necessary, sued or represented clients who were being sued. Criminal matters came up infrequently and were usually low-level affairs, typically handled without a trial, and rarely prison, although there were instances where a stint behind bars was required for a client or two. When not at his office, John would often be seen loping, sometimes in agony, to the Town Hall, where court was held, even when there was no court business, using the opportunity to converse with Mayor Baker or other town officials, all of whom, like himself, were prominent in the new Republican Party. John, of course, was very involved in local, state and even national politics and had worked very hard for the Republican cause through the fall of 1876.

*****

Into this placid, even phlegmatic, rhythm of village life, there transpired an event of such an explosive nature that, not only was the entire local populace immediately galvanized by the blaze of news, but the sparks also reached Boston and environs faster than a wildfire and would soon ignite a global conflagration. The first flicker of the inferno reached John early on the morning of November 8, delivered by his good friend, the mayor. John assumed the unscheduled visit was related to news of the election, the polling for which having concluded the night before, but of this misapprehension he was quickly disabused.

"There's been a shocking incident, John," the mayor began hurriedly following a perfunctory greeting. "The Barclays have been brutally murdered. Both were struck several times with an axe and are now quite mutilated, almost unrecognizable. It was a brutal, almost bestial, act. I am told the murder scene is disturbing beyond expression. The constabulary are there now, collecting evidence, but they have already placed the greatest suspicion on the elder daughter, Martha."

"What have they found that points to her?" John asked mechanically, his mind only slowly beginning to grasp the calamitous nature of the information being proffered.

"Well, they found the murder weapon in the fruit cellar, but of course that doesn't narrow it down. It was mostly the way she answered questions. They said her demeanor was too calm, too poised. The answers seemed almost rehearsed. Also, the first alibi she gave disintegrated immediately, but then she gave another and then, I believe, a third one after that."

"That doesn't sound well-rehearsed to me."

"I concur, John. It's all an unholy mess. I am quite disheartened by it all and, frankly, rather fearful of how this will affect the town. Besides the tragedy itself, this is going to make for a rather somber Thanksgiving, I fear. Christmas, too, if this drags on, which it seems likely to do."

"I couldn't agree more. But what is it you'd like me to do?"

Mayor Baker seemed slightly discomposed, now that his visit came to the main issue, his eyes darting about the room – taking in the furniture, the rug, the daguerreotypes and cabinet cards on the desk and bureau, the artwork on the walls, indeed just about everything except John himself – as he struggled to come to his difficult task.

"Frankly speaking, John, the scuttlebutt is that there may be a political angle here. The town's pretty Republican at this point – much thanks to you and your daddy of course – but the Barclays were strong Tilden supporters, as you know. It will be weeks before we know the outcome of yesterday's election, but all the indications we hear are that it is going to be rather problematic. I'm just concerned that all of this is going to get political. This town doesn't need another dust-up on that front."

"I couldn't agree more, Benjamin, but I'm still not certain what you want *me* to do."

"Why, I want you to turn the case down! The Barclays aren't even in the ground, and there's already a faction forming."

"Seems awfully sudden for an undertaking of that sort, don't you think?"

"It's an unholy mess, John. Especially with everything else going on with this damned election. I know the Barclays were your clients and your daddy's before you. And even if they weren't, well, hell and damnation, John, you're the only show in town, and, in addition, it's well known that you've a history of championing errant causes. She'll come to you – that's for certain – and I suppose what I'm asking as a favor is that you tell her to go to Springfield… or Boston even. I'm sure you can recommend someone. They'll get a change of venue, and we'll be well out of it. Given the whole issue with the Barclays, even before this, the entire procedure has the potentiality of getting… well, disreputable, if I can put it that way. Why, the press has already started to gather like vultures!"

John rubbed his chin thoughtfully, always a convenient aid to cogitation. He had no illusions about Robert Barclay's character, but his brain was slow in putting the pieces together on what should have been a self-obvious implication of a collective political and civic discomfiture.

"Well, Benjamin, I'd like to oblige, I surely would, but it goes against my principles as an attorney, not to mention my oath. You know I'm obligated to take the case if she comes to me."

"I can prevent that. And then there's nothing on you."

"Now, Benjamin, it has to be her choice. No blandishments, my friend. Promise me."

The mayor left with the acrid tang of that promise biting his tongue.

*****

The constabulary's initial report indicated that Robert Barclay was slaughtered in the sitting-room of his capacious home by several vicious blows to the head with an axe. Subsequent to this violent act, it appeared that no one had entered that room until several hours later, as the evidence showed, Elizabeth Barclay wandered in and almost immediately suffered the same fate. An axe, ostensibly the murder weapon, was found, stained liberally with blood, in the lowest level of the Barclay home. The time of Mr. Barclay's death was put at a dark, quiet moment in the early reaches of the day; of his wife, when the pale dawn was just giving over to the bright, chilly morn. The bodies were found by the maid, Didi O'Shaughnessy. It was her testimony to the police that proved the most damning in the case, insisting that she heard Martha arguing with her step-father the day before; that they had quarreled frequently; that Martha frequently complained to her mother of her distressing situation in the house; that her mother was dismissive of such complaints; that she knew both mother and step-father to be devoted and loving parents; that Robert Barclay was truly – despite the rumors she'd heard and openly resented – a kind, generous and affectionate parent.

The coroner's inquest was set for November 10. Even on such short notice, Storm River flooded with reporters from as far away as New York, the town virtually creaking at the seams, a dam ready to burst. As the mayor had predicted and feared, Martha reached out the very day he had spoken to John, to the only lawyer she knew. She was visibly upset, insisted on her innocence, prayed that Mr. Moulton represent her, but was otherwise distinguishably incoherent. The coroner refused – for reasons that were never made completely clear – to allow counsel at the inquest. John, having other issues and cases to attend to, did not dispute the decision, although he was to regret it exceedingly upon hearing a report of the event and, especially later, upon reading the transcript. In order to calm Martha, Doc Farlington – at the request of the coroner – dosed her rather significantly with laudanum, the natural deleterious effect of the medicine causing her testimony to appear disjointed and equivocal, the result being that all who witnessed the young woman's performance came away with a palpable impression of guilt.

The investigation conducted by Constable Oates was as slow and stodgy as the constable himself, constituting a thorough examination of the Barclay home, though finding little more than the blood stains and axe which had been discovered the first day, the interview with the maid and a few neighbors, and nothing else of any significance. News of the murders, having by now reached well beyond New England, filled the citizens of Storm River with emotions from dread to excitement, the latter flowing most especially amongst the juvenile element, who, delighting in anything novel and gruesome, relished most especially the town's newly won notoriety as much as their elders despised it. Caspar Moulton, never a particularly popular boy at school, was now courted by nearly every member of the younger set – even though there was not much, at this point, to reveal, his father not being particularly communicative about the case – but, having failed to glean any intelligence of value, he simply invented whatever he construed would provide the greatest amount of titillation to the young "cranks" suddenly clamoring for his attention. Whilst enjoying his temporary renown, Caspar nonetheless turned red with rage when informed that they were not to go to his Aunt Anna's for Thanksgiving in North Brookfield, as they usually did.

"I'm sorry, son, but with this Barclay business, I really can't leave town right now."

Caspar responded by spending even more time away from home, wandering, with his ever-present slingshot, the gentle knolls and hillocks beyond the pleasant greensward west of town. Much of the citizenry was dismayed to discover more dead birds and squirrels in the west weald – some now rather mutilated – but no one said anything, despite the general cognizance pervading the close-knit community of the derelict parent's willful ignorance.

Trial was set for February 24, 1877, as that was the earliest that Judge Garfield could make it from Boston. The weather turned suddenly quite cold before Thanksgiving, everyone predicting one of the most brutal winters ever. Whilst the holiday had only recently been cemented in national legislation, Storm River, like most towns in Massachusetts, had a long tradition of giving thanks with a sumptuous meal and numerous civic activities, but the close to this year's November was muted and tense. A caustic, brown hush settled over the entire region, even as the newsmen filed away until their inevitable return in the New Year.

*****

"We think it's an open-and-shut case, John," said Andrew Endicott, the prosecutor, traveling from his home in Boston. He had stopped in for what was purported to be a friendly visit, beginning as such with a solicitous exchange of the usual holiday greetings. Advent had just begun, and the calendar was bearing down on the solstice like a run-away sled. All New England was coated in a glacial white serene from snowfall after snowfall. Those venturing out did so in furs and blankets, crunching, if not riding on, the snow's welcome mat of winter, their breath as visible as the clouds, their noses red and wet as a musty dog's.

"Can I convince you to take a guilty plea and help prevent a ruckus at trial? I think I can promise you she won't get the death penalty with a guilty plea."

Ruckus indeed, with an advanced warning that the members of the press from as far away as San Francisco were preparing a descent upon the town set to rival Sherman's on Atlanta, causing no small amount of irritation for many of the town residents whilst the remainder responded with the cold indifference of which only a New Englander is truly capable. Storm River was, however, not the only community upended by the spectacle. With the date of the trial set, every inn from Springfield to Bedford Falls was swimming in reservation requests for the latter half of February, with gripes and groans registering from the green-grocer's to the smithy. With most of the prosecution's case based on the testimony of an Irish maid, there was even interest shown in the Emerald Isle, one of whose "penny papers" sent a member whiffling across the ocean well ahead of time to the general disapproval of the considerable Puritan element of the town. And, as everyone knew – even those with less worldly experience than John and Andrew – the curiosity seekers would follow the newsmen as winter follows fall.

John and Andrew were old friends from John's time in Boston, but, that being said, John was not prepared to capitulate just to please him.

"Well, Andrew, I know it's your job to offer such an attractive deal, but I think on the whole, we're going to trial. I have spoken to my client numerous times, and there is no inclination there to accept these crimes as hers. I know this pains you, but gird your loins because we are going into battle, my friend, so prepare to spar once again."

Clearly trying not to prick or sting, John was attempting to keep the tone light and airy, yet it was indubitably a distasteful interview for him with such an old friend as Andrew. Sadly, Andrew, seemingly under some covert pressure, was not making the confrontation easy, cajoling and wheedling the point for nearly an hour, little knowing the terrible strain he was exacting on his old friend. After the disconcerting scene, John was compelled to increase his dose another ten drops that evening, just to deaden the raw impact of the discussion. He slept in starless depths and could not easily be roused in the morning by the gentle Vesta, who had come to inform him that Caspar once again had failed to return home until quite late, undoubtedly roaming the nether parts of town and the tulgey grove just beyond, like a malignant wraith under crystalline heavens.

Christmastime was typically a season of simple but heartfelt celebration in Storm River, centered on community gatherings, church services, the joyful enactments of family traditions, and the rigorous manifestations of nature-inspired decorations. The town itself presented a charming scene, despite the looming precipice of the trial, with gas lamps glowing warmly under the cold crescent moon, illuminating the snow-strewn cobblestone streets and tidy houses, which, decorated with evergreen wreaths tied with red ribbons, stood proudly against the frosty air, while small candles in windows signaled Christmas cheer and warmth within.

Most families gathered to prepare handmade ornaments, frequently accompanied by dried fruits, popcorn garlands, or little wax figures to hang on their trees. Christmas trees in Storm River, typically small – really no more than saplings gently cut from the local forest surrounding the bucolic town – were placed in most homes on tables to showcase carefully crafted decorations of pinecones, holly, and mistletoe, along with handmade gifts placed around the base, forming the locus of the simple beauty of each domicile.

Christmastide 1876 at the Moulton home, however, saw little cheer. The house remained overcast with work and neglect, and the customary annual trip to Turner Creek to spend the holidays with John's sister Rachel's family was also rudely dismissed. If Caspar enjoyed time with the Fuller family at Thanksgiving, he especially liked Christmas with his cousins in Turner Creek, making this second loss for the boy a tenebrous irritation. John's habit of returning from the office at the dark end of a short day, dosing and going to bed, always increased during the Christmas season, at least until they left for his sister's home, but with no Yuletide journey this year – and a highly consequential case hanging over him like the mythical sword – John's dosing simply increased as the nights grew longer and the darkness deepened. Decorations, presents, and celebrations were left this year entirely in the hands of the competent Vesta, but, absent any homey activities, were a small source of comfort for, and therefore control over, the gloomy and increasingly feral Caspar. It was not that John was in utter denial of his son's shady activities, but his own throbbing soul quite simply lacked the capacity to fathom the caliginous depths to which the boy's dudgeon could plunge, nor to accept his spirit redounding to any truly evil activity. Further, whenever his thoughts trailed from such murky disillusionment, the compassionate Vesta was certain to attempt enlightenment, but John simply assumed that the loss of maternal love had encrueled his son's soul – much as the loss of conjugal love had mutilated his own – and that the only savior for his progeny would be some far away phrontistery to which he would certainly be consigned in but a few years' time, thus averting his long-term problem while leaving him free to toil away at the current issue of the trial.

*****

The New Year jolted its way to New England on piercing cold and inky clouds, obstructing the night's beauty and the sun's gleam, its regular morning task to awaken the fragile, benumbed counselor, aided by the faithful Vesta, who found herself this morning overwhelmed by the arrival of an early, icy-eyed brigade of concerned citizenry demanding to see that disconcerted gentleman. This solemn regiment included the mayor and several other prominent men of the town, a phalanx of respectable, taut humanity who, the dedicated housemaid feared, were coming to complain about the activities of the young man for whom she was, by default, the sole caretaker, especially as it included the Right Reverend Lowell, not a customary attendee of the political platoon that had been meeting with greater regularity since the irregular outcome of the recent presidential contest. She led them diffidently into the large parlor and proceeded to the now complicated quotidian process of rousing the master of the house, taking the care a sailor might in hoisting sails, flags or spars.

"We heard the prosecutor offered young Martha a nice deal for a guilty plea," Mayor Baker started off when John finally made his appearance after an amount of time many in the group found excessive. "Second degree with no death penalty."

"I'm afraid she isn't interested in spending the rest of her life in prison, Benjamin. She's only twenty-seven, gentlemen. Life imprisonment is not much of an alternative, especially since she is innocent."

Selectman Peabody was not as convinced as the defense attorney. "Oh, John, please excuse me, but that is not the general impression, especially of those such as myself who have considered the issue closely. No one wants this brought up, of course, especially as it paints the town rather badly for overlooking the issue, and indeed my sympathies are with the poor girl, excuse me Reverend Lowell as well, but we all know what kind of man Barclay was--"

"Damned Democrat scum, if you ask me," piped in old Tom Bartlett.

"That's not what I was alluding to, as you know, and we agreed to keep politics out of this despite what those devils in Washington are up to."

"I understand the argument for justifiable homicide," John drawled slowly, with a hasty glance at the reverend, "but, again, gentlemen, no disrespect intended, that is not her story. And, frankly, I am fairly confident of getting her off entirely. The prosecution's case, at least so far, is entirely circumstantial."

"Maybe if you agreed to a changed venue. Andrew said you opposed that. I can't imagine why."

John Moulton fidgeted a bit in thinking of an answer, trying to ensure it did not have the fragrance of a gripe. His leg felt inflamed and throbbed with vexatious protraction; his head felt dull and clotted; his hands seemed to have doubled in size, and he found it an arduous task simply holding his coffee cup without spilling.

"I can't try this case a hundred miles from here. I can't leave here."

The silence in the room took on the weight of the assorted heavy thoughts of the assemblage, each man ascribing a different impetus for the defense attorney's reticence, the group forming a tacit cleavage between those who were aware – if not specifically, then at least in a general way – of the medication he imbibed, and those who thought his concern was for leaving his son in the hands of the young Negress, for various reasons – not the least of which the young gentleman's nocturnal habits – with a few disrespectful speculations muttered regarding his reluctance to leave the housemaid at all; though all who gathered were close, or at least not terribly distant, friends – all stout Republicans with a strong appreciation of all the Moulton family as a whole had done for town, state, and country – some had none-the-less allowed a quiet ear to bend to the disgusting gossip regarding the lawyer and the dusky woman who toiled beneath his roof.

"Look here, John. I'm going to come out and say what these gentlemen are afraid of saying," said Selectman Smith. "To prove her not guilty, you're going to have to point to someone else for the murders. Who the devil's it going to be?"

The atmosphere in the room went from merely tense to practically crackling with the electricity of a thunderstorm, the tangible version of which seemed to be advancing from the northeast. As John chose not to respond – either through an unwillingness to share his thoughts on the matter or because he had never given it any consideration – the silence was especially incommodious, dissolving slowly from its icy wall into a trickling flow of murmuration, with Reverand Lowell continuing to stand silently apart out of his noble sense of Christian decorum. One looked at another with a nod and a stare, each hoping from the other some sort of compromise out of the impasse, when Selectman Davis chose to ease things by coming with a different drift.

“See, the thing is, John, that the Barclays were strong Tilden supporters, as Tom has referenced here. Well, with all that’s going on and the uncertainty of how it’s going to be resolved in Washington – you know Zachary is already on his way there with the Massachusetts delegation to work things out – well, John, the concern amongst many of us is whether or not this might not become a political issue. There is an element in this town that would love to see this as Republican rage. We want to avoid that.”

“It was never my intention of getting political in the courtroom, Winslow,” John responded calmly, “and I hope you gentlemen don’t take me for ‘a sockdologizing old man-trap’”.

If John had expected the comic quotation to lighten the tableau, he had failed miserably, the sardonic color of the phrase having been darkened by its tragic reference, investing a mordant patina that could not be whitewashed by his subsequent wry smile. Silence descended like an umber pall, several of the men wondering if the allusion was meant as a deliberate rebuke. Indeed, some commented later on the whole picture having been drawn in poor taste, many quietly opining that it emerged from an opiated palette while others referenced openly the poor quality of what should be every father’s most important portraiture. The tragically comic phrase continued to pervade the room like an ill-timed, involuntary petard of peculiar pungency, and the wry smile John engineered to dispel the odor – or at least to perform the services of a nosegay until the moment passed – was seen by the least sympathetic of his listeners as a nasty smirk while his closer friends assumed it was another grimace of agony. In the protracted silence that followed, it was left to John himself to air the room.

“I know you gentlemen only mean the best… for Martha, for the town and yes, even for me,” John continued. “I know there is some real concern there. I’d have to be a fool not to. To speak frankly amongst friends, there is no reason to bring up any issue regarding Roberts’s – what shall I say? – *attitude* toward young Martha, not to mention poor Emma as well. There is no reason to bring the election madness into it either. And I assure you all, despite the medicaments necessary to ease the trouble of my old wound, I am perfectly capable of navigating Martha Simpson’s defense without drama or incident. I assure you, my good friends and neighbors, if this case runs into troubled waters, it will not be I who piloted it there.”

Whispers and nods, with a few shakes of the head, carried the room, whilst others, previously silent, continued unable to find suitable comment, until John himself offered that, if they had serious concerns, those could be taken up with the judge in the case. With that unanswered recommendation, the committee left in a dignified recession.

*****

Nothing untoward occurred, as John indicated, either during v*oir dire* or in opening statements. The courtroom, as expected, was packed like an overnight valise containing a fortnight's worth of clothing, spilling out from the Town Hall into the square, with neighbors, inquisitive tourists, and the press straining to get a slim glimpse of the freakish young woman who – all had apparently decided – so violently ended her family. The prosecutor laid out his case simply, and the defense attorney laid out his, with perhaps a bit more emotion, in slow, deliberate sentences and solemn stares at the jury. Forensic evidence, such as there was, was presented clearly and was unchallenged while all further aspects of the trial proceeded in complete order and with a general spirit of comity, until it was time for Dierdre Sullivan to give her testimony.

Andrew Endicott called Miss Sullivan to the stand with especial gravity, this being the very crux of his argument. He led her through her previous testimony with the skill and precision of a well-practiced surgeon who could remove a leg in a trice. The young Irish maid, for her part, answered each inquiry with clear green eyes and a lovely lilt that seemed to beguile the gentlemen of the jury despite the gruesome nature of the subject-matter. John began his cross-examination in a gentlemanly fashion – noting that the witness had carried the room with her graceful Celtic charm – wearing a congenial smile of his own which he hoped would put her at ease.

"Now, Miss Sullivan, you testified that you heard raised voices the night before."

"Yes, sir."

"And, although you could not see them, you clearly recognized the voice of my client, Martha Simpson, and her mother and stepfather?"

"Yes, sir."

"Can you be certain it was truly my client and not her sister, Emma?

"Yes, sir."

"Truly? They sound very similar. In fact, we are prepared to bring witnesses who know the family quite well to say that they cannot tell the difference between the two sisters' voices. How can you be so certain?"

"Well… I was pretty sure Emma wasn't--"

"I'm sorry for interrupting, my good woman, but 'pretty sure' is not really admissible here when we are looking for something beyond a reasonable doubt."

"Well, then, sir, I would say I know beyond a reasonable doubt that Emma was not in the house at the time. I saw her leave earlier to go to the Freemans."

"Do you know for certain that she had not returned at that point in time?"

"No, sir," she responded after a short pause, "I cannot say for certain."

John managed to further disconcert the now flummoxed maid into admitting that there had been frequent arguments between Martha and her parents, "and none of those instances resulted in murder, had they?" No, indeed, they had not.

The precise measurement of the self-administered dose John imbibed following that disagreeable cross-examination can never be known for certain, given the abject state in which he returned to his office. Vesta made dinner for Caspar and attempted, as she did most evenings, to get him to apply the appropriate attention to his studies. She had even, earlier in the week, taken on the implicitly maternal occupation of speaking with the teacher to glean any advice on how to proceed with the miserable and increasingly wrathful truant. But Caspar preferred playing outside with his slingshot and Vesta lacked the parental authority to bring him to heel. She placed the knitted throw over John and let him sleep on the sofa, a slovenly habit he had been cultivating more and more of late.

*****

March arrived in its classical leonine manner, Typhon trailing in its wake with an angry profusion of sleet and bitter winds tormenting all, despite their long custom of harsh transitions inherent with the vernal month. Town Hall was filled long before the judge was due to gavel in the final day of the trial, filling the courtroom with the cold steam customarily released by combined humanity in crowded quarters humidly heated. The commotion of the gallery mirrored the equinoctial tempest raging throughout New England, and, indeed, the nation, as the ship of state foundered in its own procellous sea to a final, perilous surge, the conclusion and compromise of the quadrennial contest to determine who will steer a nation that still bled from open wounds of war and the vain stitchings of Reconstruction.

John now faced the most crucial question of the trial: whether or not to put Martha on the stand. The girl's pitiable testimony, especially in contrast to the impetuous gale outdoors, could clinch her freedom, but a wrong word, gesture, or glance could just as easily, in an instant, dish her chances of seeing the next summer sun. His brain, long clouded by pain that ebbed and flowed with the exertions of walking and the application of liquid relief, while also dealing with its own desperate exasperation, struggled to determine a categorical conclusion. In the end, he decided that he did not require her testimony and that chancing her ability to charm the jury – especially after Didi's performance – was too great a risk. It is true he was counting, to an extent he found weirdly discomfiting, on the jury's sympathy, keenly knowledgeable as he was of the personalities of the jurors, but given the size and nature of the town – a place where gossip and information of various levels of reliability flowed like the torrential rapids of a swift stream – Storm River was quite simply a place where everyone knew everyone else and pretty much everything, even if they knew it prejudicially or imperfectly, and thus, at least for an advocate of an unpopular cause, made the entire enterprise wretchedly unpredictable. As for the trial itself and Martha's part in the matter, the residents of that previously equable town had been rather evenly divided on the subject – almost its own little playact of the blue and the gray – but as the trial proceeded and news spread, John felt the sympathy of crowd bending in a gentle arc toward Justice. In an act, therefore, of unadulterated optimism and with every anticipation of success, he concluded that such goodwill extended to the twelve gentlemen he had faced each day that week. Besides, the longer the trial dragged on, the more detrimental it was to his health.

The prosecution's summing up took less than an hour. He reviewed all the facts of the case and leaned heavily on Didi's relatively unbroken testimony. The judge called a recess for lunch. John retired to his office and lunched lightly on a cheese sandwich and a mug of hot cider, which the loyal Vesta brought to him from the corner saloon. His leg was cramping more than usual, even for a winter day of such tempestuous rage, when the cold penetrated deep, exacerbating the ever-present throb down his limb and even into the groin. He feared the jurors would notice the change to his gait caused by the incessant and increasing pain, so, when he had finished eating, he allowed himself a small dose, in desperation, to allow him to pace, as he naturally did in his summations, but kept it light, aware of the necessity to remain fully alert and as lucid as a fair summer sky.

After calling the room to order, the judge nodded to John who rose to his feet slowly, ponderously, with a slightly more flavescent pallor, and with great deliberation and solemnity.

"Our community has been rocked and shattered by a terrible and violent crime. Two respected members of our community were brutally murdered with an axe. Of this, there is no doubt. But it is the only thing about this case where there is no doubt. Even the supposed murder weapon, a common household tool, found in any lodging in our community, or, indeed in any domicile in any New England town, was not definitively shown to be *the* axe that did the grisly deed.

"We know the time and place of the deaths, true, but the exact time is uncertain. There is a time range. That is the best the coroner could do. This is not an attempt to impugn the honorable doctor's testimony. He is certainly giving the best answer modern medical knowledge can attest to. But medicine is not an exact science, and he cannot give an exact time. And, as we have shown, our client, the defendant, Miss Martha Simpson, was fast asleep for most of that time range.

"The prosecution has shown definitively that my client had the strength to wield the alleged murder weapon in a manner effective enough to crush the skull. But the first victim was facing his assailant at the time the blow was struck. Is it really believable that, seeing his stepdaughter approaching him in a threatening manner, with an axe raised high, that he would have simply stood there and allowed it to happen? Wouldn't a man of Mr. Barclay's size and strength put up an adequate enough fight to fend off a delicate young lady?

"The case is distressing, gentlemen of the jury. Distressing for the family, for the community, indeed, given the interest of the members of the press here in the courtroom and outside, for the entire Commonwealth. I will share with you that it is personally quite vexing to me as well. So, I understand that there is certainly a strong desire to close the book on this and get on with our lives. We don't want to admit that an innocent person has been arrested. We don't want to think that a murderer is still out there at large, with no inkling as to who it is. We don't want to know these uncomfortable things. But do we really rather wish to believe that this horrific crime was committed by a fragile maiden who has lived in our midst all of our lives?

"Not with the scanty evidence the prosecutor has brought to this trial. No! I personally would not like to send this fine young woman, our friend and neighbor, Miss Martha Simpson, to her death based only on circumstantial evidence and hearsay. And I trust that all you gentlemen – men I too have known all my life – will feel the same. Look at her, gentlemen. Look at my client, our neighbor, and ask yourselves, deep in your hearts, whether or not you know, beyond a reasonable doubt, gentlemen, that this fine young woman, who has lived amongst us since a babe, would have done this thing, this brutal, bestial thing of which she is accused. I am confident, if you look to your hearts, you will find the defendant not guilty and will allow her to live as best she can after the shattering of her family."

*****

It had taken everything out of him. Beginning his limp home, Ed Jenkins kindly offered him a ride in his cabriolet. John, as a rule, was too proud to accept such an indulgence – despite his injury, he always insisted on walking to his office or the Town Hall, allowing each pang and twinge to serve as a reminder of sacrifice and honor – but considering the toll taken on his soul in addition to his corporeal self, to say nothing of the bite of the blustery northeast wind with its blinding chips of ice, he reluctantly assented. Upon his arrival, he asked Vesta if Caspar was home and received the intelligence that school was still in session. Whether the lad was at school or not, Vesta did not know and did not say, but he was certainly not expected home until nearly suppertime, especially as sundown now succeeded the evening meal.

Assuming the jury would be out for quite some time, John took it upon himself to administer the maximum dose of sixty drops, though, as it nearly depleted his supply, he decided that emptying the bottle entirely would not be detrimental and might even be beneficial. He knew he stored more of the essential elixir at the office but made a mental note to see Doc Jenkins in Swampscott for another fillip. He hadn't applied to him in well over a month and felt assured the good doctor would oblige.

As the numbing wave swept over him, his musings rocked from the maelstrom of the trial to the gentler stream of uffish musings on a shaded past, recent and long ago, the Cimmerian depths of which he normally did not plumb. As he wondered what the future held for Martha Simpson, a dizzying array of quiddities, quillities, soccages, and writs gyrated in a vertiginous progression of elucidatory questions he recalled having failed to ask during the trial. As he ransacked his recent memories, which flowed from Party meetings – filled with the desperation for a brighter tomorrow for his nation and for the still half-enslaved people drowning in a precarious freedom that cost so many so dearly, especially the bloodbath of Antietam – and the transformative task thus now inherent, to the moment he found poor Vesta, shivering half-naked, bewailing a husband and child beaten to death before her eyes, that baleful figure, like a changeling in dreams, blanching into Sarah, the delicious face that filled his nights and days, a panorama of the life they had planned and the one God chose instead to deliver, and to which he, like many before him, and many since, most assuredly, would need to succumb. As the pain of his loss stupefied his dream, he floated on to Caspar, his beaming lighthouse and benighted chasm, his illimitable joy and eternal sore, his binding to the mast of conjugality blending to an amalgamate as an estuary conjoins to a brackish miasma, even as the truant himself was roaming the fetid copses and noisome bracken on the city's edge. As agitation battled remorse and his addled spirit went galumphing through inchoate vistas of shrieking tremors, breaking the bonds of sobriety, escaping the burden of tangibility, he fought to gain the soft, exquisite tenderness of oblivion, to feel on his face the chill of other stars, to swim the discourse of an ungirt pleasure, lank and dilute, to propitiate the unencumbered, to shout away the languid hull of his shattered, purposeless life, the hurtful modulation of which now nothing more than a quiet bleat or a silent scream. As the nubilous cogitation persisted, his thoughts took on colors and textures, sounds and odors, unlike any previous visitations, a diaphanous flotilla of pink clouds, the gaze of a velvet sky sprinkled with faery dust, vivid as decay, pungent as darkness, with hellish blasts of a blustery fire transported to the pit of a winter's night.

Distant knocking seemed to bubble up from the depths of a forest, the sensation of trees being felled by hack and hew, powerful strokes in a desperate petition, curling down the street, whisking up the stairs and invading his bedroom, propitiating a disillusioned mob of miscreants with the smooth vitality of release. If he heard his name distilled in the sinking repetition of coarse paintings or the imprecation conjuring a return of fury, it was merely combined with the music of dawn, the cramp of sunlight, animal cries of night-night chortling in his mind's ear, an intonation of such cacophony where no melody could be discerned. Some tiny speck of knowledge must have invaded his wandering soul as the vision of Martha intersected with the malediction of her damnable parents, whose visages coalesced above the foam – now whole and now slashed and smashed – the vibration of the wooden handle discernable through the splintering of one skull after another, blood and guts and ouns washing away with the viscous tide of a savage lust for vengeance, of justice delayed and freedom denied, of a desperate instauration of decency and safety for lost and persecuted children, for a country adrift, and for the swirling tide of an ebony humanity, so long abused, oppressed and despised in their own homes.

But why kick against the pricks of power if the routine flow of events, either abaft or abeam, is nothing but a turbid procession of black bilge, searing from the soul, the putridity of the rotting bodies of the dead upon dead in a sunken road? As much as John was able to bring his consciousness to wrestle with the problem, the persistent vision of sweet Vesta, the woman he saved, the woman who saved him, floated above, gazing through snowfalls, reaching with her slim, brown arms from a distended form undulating in a salacious bath of fluorescent delectation; lovely Vesta, the pitching sloop of transcendent felicity at the brave mercy of supple hands, a silky relief from his enervating immiseration. If he'd felt those self-same hands shaking him gently and then with greater exaction – desperate to rouse, to raise, to kindle – joined by others, more forceful, it seemed like nothing other than the placid lolling of a drunken tar in the hold of a ghostly ship, clambering, floundering and chiming determinedly in its piercing, agonizing pitch and yaw, while lumbering – as such pixilated wrecks might do in the face of gale-ridden skullduggery – desperate to disencumber the dreadful, dingy cataclysm of corporeality, and fade, without knowledge, without consequence, without arousal, without the decency of intendment, without any sense of divine ubiety, without everything, into its ultimate terminus, its final welcomed port of call.

One Fine Day

January 25, 1995

"Is this a gay bar?"

"Yeah. You have a problem with that?"

"No. I just didn't know you were a lesbian now."

"I'm not. I just like this place. My girlfriends and I come here 'cause it's quiet and we don't get hit on."

"Don't you get hit on by girls?"

"Not when I'm with my girlfriends. Are you uncomfortable?"

"Well, a little."

"Well, if you're that concerned, you can come over here, and we can make out. That should keep you safe, eh?"

"It's not that. It's just because it isn't our element. Don't they resent us being in their space?"

"*I've* never felt that way."

Peter Covert and Maggie Nichols were seated in a quiet corner of Chez Moi. The pub, located in a latent cul-de-sac just a block off Yonge and Bloor, was a few steps down with the bar near the entrance and a large dance floor in the middle surrounded by tables and booths. The music was canned, though subdued, but no one was listening or dancing. The room was half-full, dotted with seated couples or milling singles. The lighting was low, as much as to keep the Hydro bill down as to accommodate private intimacies.

Maggie had secured the first round at the bar while Peter read the menu card as he settled into the booth. It was sometime later, while noticing an acquaintance eyeing him thoughtfully from a table several meters away as the waiter delivered the third round, that the epiphany of their surroundings hit him. He had to admit that he was more comfortable where their conversation had started earlier in the evening, at The Brunswick House, a far larger, brighter, and noisier venue. The reporters for the University of Toronto's student newspaper, *The Varsity*, who had spent the day covering student protests, met there for a round-up over several pitchers of what was purportedly Molsen's Ale.

"It's total bullshit!"

"Not if we write it up properly."

"Nothing's going to happen. Nothing ever happens."

"You know there was a similar protest back in the early 70's. Demonstrations. Students getting fined for withholding tuition. Sit-ins. Marches. Everything. Did it do any good? Here we are again, eh?"

"Totally."

The Brunswick House on any given night was loud, discordant, and thick with smoke. Conversation interrupted conversation shouted above the ribald singing and intemperate raucousness of this fine establishment, known more for cheap beer than quiet ambience. The beer, poured from large pitchers, frequently missed the glasses, and the floor was sticky with a history no one wanted to clean. Students from the university, their pockets light and their hearts heavy with tendentious concerns, mixed with the old men and women who had been there since long before these kids were born. The felt-worn pool tables in the back hadn't been balanced since they were installed, and the ancient jukebox played a song by The Chiffons few there would recognize. A man with a face like an apathetic apricot leaned on the bar, and the bartender, a woman who had seen much and cared less, filled another pitcher. Outside, the cold streetlights flickered, but inside, under the warm yellow incandescent glow, the warm yellow watered-down beer kept coming. The night pressed on, thick and endless, like all the Wednesday nights before it.

"Hold on! Hold on!" Bruce, the editor, shouted as he poured himself another. "We're not here to determine the outcome but to report the story."

"The story is that this is total bullshit," Tanya repeated.

"I see that as our headline," Conan jumped in: "*National Day of Action: Total Bullshit!*"

"It's not funny, Val," Tanya complained to her laughing friend. "How are we going to change things if we don't take a stand?"

"We change things by doing our job and reporting the truth."

"C'mon, Bruce, there is no objective 'truth,' and you know it," Natasa chimed in with air quotes. "Just read the same story in *The Star* and in *The Globe and Mail,* and you can see that!"

"Truth may not be objective, but *we* can be objective, eh?"

"That's a rather fine distinction."

"Look, we can either–"

"Let's do round-up," said Bruce, calling the meeting to order. Each person was to go over the story they had covered. It was then that Maggie nudged Peter with a nod and a wink that got him to leave. "It'll just be a rehash of this morning and it's too loud in here to talk. I know a better place."

The morning's review that was about to be rehashed had begun early, long before sunrise, as the student reporters crowded into the paper's hot, cramped editorial office while Bruce Corcoran handed out the assignments.

"The march is planned down Wellesley, so we'll need someone on the corner of Wellesley and Bay to interview. Val, you can handle that."

"Check."

"Helen, I want you to follow up your piece on the other universities. Stay in touch with your contacts at Western, Dalhousie, McGill–"

"I think Quebec's sitting this one out."

"Fine. You know how to handle that, eh?"

"Yep. Totally gassed."

"Thanks, Helen. Daria, your piece on the suburban response was great, but you can't cover Erindale *and* Scarborough. Pick one."

"Scarborough," she responded without a pause.

"Fine, then Maggie, you take Erindale."

"Bullshit, Bruce. I'm not going way out there."

"C'mon, Maggie, don't be such a prima donna. Daria doesn't mind."

"Daria didn't have a summer internship at *The Star* with a job offer for after graduation. C'mon, Bruce, you gotta put me closer to the action."

"Okay, how about UC? They were the third college to endorse the strike, eh?"

"You hoser! I want Convocation Hall."

"Sorry. Laura's getting Con Hall."

"That's *peak* bullshit."

Maggie was short and blonde and cute and from the tiny town of Moosonee in Ontario's far north, so, having learned at a young age to take care of herself, she was determined to not take shit from anyone. In an earlier age, she would have been known as a "firecracker." This did not make her popular on campus nor especially at the newspaper. As a result, the room erupted when she laid out her demands.

"Hold it down. Hold it *down*," Bruce said, stopping the commotion. "Jeez! … Maggie, you're a terrific writer, and you'll make a great journo, but you need to accept directions. Now, I agreed to keep you on main campus, but that's as far as I go. You cover UC or you're off. Decide."

She decided and Bruce moved on.

"Fine, so Maggie's got UC, Laura's got Con Hall, and David, you're at SAC, right? Fine, you take that. Pete, you okay with talking to students who don't participate?"

"Fine."

"Appreciate that, Pete."

And on it went. Everyone agreed to meet at "The Bruns for a coupla cool wet ones" when it was over. The day was as long, exciting and tiring as expected. Peter had finished his task early, having completed nearly twenty interviews before noon. Knowing he had enough juicy quotes in his notebook, he sat out the remains of the day. Writing his article would be no problem. Maggie, predictably, had gone off-roading (presumably why Bruce had tried to keep her thirty kilometers from the main action), going through the colleges on main campus like a hyper-potent enema, interviewing, observing and filling two-and-a-half notebooks with intense jottings. She was the last to arrive at The Bruns. The post-protest meeting grew boisterous even before the first pitchers had arrived. Bruce was dismayed to see Pete and Maggie leave prior to giving their reports, but decided it was better to let them slide. As long as they filed their stories Friday morning in time for the Monday edition.

On the walk to Chez Moi, Maggie vented further on the situation while Pete listened quietly. The snow crunched under their boots as they walked along Bloor Street, the cold pressing in, the wind finding the gaps in their coats. Maggie's words spilled out in a quick, unbroken stream – about the students at Vic, the profs at Innis, the commotion at Hart House, the excitement of seeing thousands of students supported by thousands more, all braving the weather and potential repercussions, fighting for what was fair and just and fine and true. He nodded, listening meekly, hands in his pockets, contemplating how their breaths exhaled in white billows and the way the frost made the streetlamps look like dubious moons. She went on, earnestly, intently, rarely breaking for a laugh, until, finally catching herself, she stopped.

He walked another step, maybe two, before turning back to her with a questioning glance.

"I've been talking too much," she said. He looked at her, then shook his head. "It's fine," he said. But it wasn't fine with her, so as they picked up pace again, she decided to open him up.

"Doesn't it mean anything to you?"

"Well, if you're talking about the assignments, no, not really. It's not like I plan to do this as a living, like you. I mean, I totally get why it was important to you, but …"

"But?" she asked after a pause.

"Well, I'm not planning to go into journalism like you. I do more fiction, you know. I'm just working at the Varg for larks… and my resumé, of course."

"By fiction, you mean like potboilers like Hugh MacLennan's *Barometer Rising*?"

"Jeezo, that's a blast from the past. Maybe something with more art to it, like Basil Jackson's *Epicenter*. A thriller about the dangers of nuclear power. Totally based on real Toronto corruption."

"Based on but not proven. That's the problem. Pickering's still up and running. No changes. A novel lets people dismiss the truth as 'just another story.' Now look at Stevie Cameron and *On the Take*. That's going to shake up the entire Mulroney government. It'll change everything. Where's the novel that can do that, eh?"

"How about *Handmaid's Tale*? It attacks the problem of religion in politics tangentially but deals with the human condition at its basis, and, again, brilliantly written. Fiction like that speaks to the heart of things, not just the surfaces. In fifty years, no one will care about Mulroney, but they *will* care about corruption in the human heart, and that's where literature can help inform understanding. People will be reading *Handmaid's Tale* long after *On the Take* is out of print."

"I know you wrote a couple of short stories last year, wasn't it? Did they go to the heart of things? You never offered to let me read them, you know."

"You never asked."

"Would you've let me if I had?"

A short dour snort escaped his nose. "Maybe not."

Their frigid walk brought them to the quieter pub where they warmed themselves over a couple of rye and gingers. Maggie continued to extoll the virtues of her chosen profession in rapid, jubilant exclamations as Peter quietly sipped his drink and munched peanuts, responding apathetically, almost flippantly at times.

"Look at the corruption in the Rosedale riding in the last election. Not much of a potboiler there, but *The Star* did a great exposé. No one would have known without good journalism exposing all of that. We can really change things. Fix society's ills, make the world a better place."

"Good literature does that. It moves people and it… *stays*! I mean, can anyone recall any newspaper article from 1865? No, but they still read *David Copperfield* and *War and Peace*. You're a terrific writer, Maggie. But you want to right wrongs where I just want to write. Is that so wrong? And to be honest, I think you should too. 'If you keep doing newspaper work'" he quoted at her, "'you'll never see things, you will only see words…'"

She smiled at the shared memory, her face softening with the pale recollection of other poignant moments, the sheen in her eyes returning the sad glow in his. They each tasted the pause while the third round was delivered, and Peter noticed the nature of the clientele. Maggie, eliding his evasion of her suggestion, drank deep and changed tack.

"Why did it never happen for us, Pete? It's like we were shooting at the same target but kept missing the mark."

"Timing, I guess. I know I was interested in you while you were going with Dan…"

"… and I was interested in you while you were with Marlene, yes, I remember. Dan! Gawd, what a Gino! But we're both free now, eh?"

"I'm not sure how free I am right now, to be honest. I feel trapped, I guess."

"Well, like I said, come shit by me and–"

"What you say?"

"I said come sit by me –"

"You said 'shit by me.'"

"Bullsit! Ha!"

"I think you've had enough."

"There's never enough for the needy or greedy… or seedy!"

Her laughter, which had punctuated their conversation like a rising tide, finally let loose in an unrestrained flood. Peter looked around apprehensively. The last thing he wanted was to attract attention and excite comment in such an awkward environment.

"I think maybe you've had enough."

"You think I can't hold my liquor?"

"True say."

"Liquor! You wanna lick 'er? HA!"

"I think it's time we headed out, eh?"

"Seriously, this place makes you nervous?"

"No, *you* make me nervous!"

"It's a vibe!"

"Jokes!"

"Both free now."

"Seriously, we've got those stories to file, and it's getting late."

"Fine fine fine *fine!* Hey! We could work on 'em together, eh? Coe-Lab-Err-Ate! My place, eh?"

"No, thanks. I'm dusted, and you're wasted. I'll see you home, though."

The walk from the pub to Maggie's place on Jarvis was long and cold. Colder than before. The wind cut at them with greater ferocity. Their steps were slow, slower than their stroll from The Bruns, and slightly less sure-footed. Maggie continued to talk. In fact, she talked the whole way. Her voice was bright at first, full of drink and laughter. But the walk, with its constant movement and cold fresh air, sobered her, moderating her garrulousness without actually ceasing the flow. With each step, her words came slower, quieter, like a fire burning low but still steadily.

"I can't wait till commencement. I am so geeked about working at *The Star*. And I can't wait to read your first novel. Are you very far into it?"

"I have it sketched out. But… I dunno…"

"What is it, Pete?"

"Well, I haven't told anyone, but my parents – my father really – want me to go to law school, so I took the LSAT and applied, and I … well, I got into Osgoode."

"Why, that's terrific, Peter!"

"No doubt. But it means giving up writing. I guess I've gotta make a decision soon, eh?"

"Well, we're talking about helping society and shit, and I'm like journalism, and you're like fiction, but as a lawyer, shit, you could be so much more impactful, eh?'

"I guess."

They reached her door and turned to each other. Maggie's face was bright and windburnt red, her eyes alive with excitement and promise, her demeanor rippling with anticipation. Peter was still concerned about her condition.

"Yeah, fine, now. Yeah, really. Thanks. I guess I *was* a bit tanked. But today was really sick, wasn't it? Seeing thousands of students protesting and fighting. Thousands, Peter! Day of Action, eh? So fine!"

"I guess. It'll be interesting to see what comes of it."

They looked at each other through the clear, frigid air. It was deep into the night by now, and the ambivalence hovering between them was as chilly as the wind. Neither one seemed to know quite how to leave things.

"You could come up, if you like.... Go over notes?"

Peter looked up into the sky as if asking the stars for an answer. He looked up and then down the empty street, and then finally into Maggie's questioning eyes.

"Nah. I don't think so. I'm really jammed up with homework."

"Okay, sure, of course, yeah, fine. No problemo, boyo. Later."

Maggie turned to clamber up the stairs. Peter watched complacently as she opened the front door. She turned to see him still at the bottom of the steps, hands in pocket, boots on the ground, looking up with an odd expression, a longing, a sense of possibility but also tinged with concern, even fear.

"You sure?" she asked, trying to read him. "I've got cocoa."

He allowed a crooked smile with another brief snort.

"Maybe another time, eh?"

"Sure, Pete. Sure. See you Monday."

"Monday, Maggs."

And with that, she disappeared. Peter remained motionless, contemplating the walk to the College subway station. Finally, shaking his head quickly and, with a mournful cadence, he turned to retrace his steps to Chez Moi.

Day Off

June 16, 1904

Whilst most New Yorkers enjoy the numerous short-sleeved pleasures of a summer's day, for domestic help in that great city, one particular beauty of the June mornings that straddle the solstice is that, no matter how early the commencement of the workday, it begins in a lambent glimmer rather than in complete darkness. This morning, the two young maids who shared the top of the sprawling brownstone on East Fourth Street awoke together, as usual, the light in the attic window just beginning to bloom with the sun's first kiss gilding the roofs of nearby buildings. Still sleepy and quiet, they washed quickly with the cool water from the pitcher on the washstand and dressed quickly, slipping quietly into plain cotton dresses, tying aprons about slim waists, and pulling hair – the elder Bridget's auburn, the younger Nora's more copper-hued – into tight buns.

"So, today's the day, yes?" Bridget asked, breaking the silence.

"Be quiet!" Nora responded quickly. "I don't know. It depends, I suppose."

"On him, or you?!"

"Oh, hush!"

They emerged quickly from their garret next to the nursery-turned-sewing-room, hurrying to a quick breakfast in the kitchen, after which they effected their morning chores – Bridget helping Cook with the Family's breakfast while Nora fetched water from the cistern, heated it, and brought a jug to each family member for their morning ablutions. That completed, she joined Bridget in the breakfast room to help prepare it for the Family's arrival. Heads together, bronze by gold, Bridget quietly took up their fourth floor's conversation where they'd left off – the elder with a coy smirk while the younger girl blushed.

The girls' muted giggling was startled by the sound of unaccustomed footsteps without. They looked at each other in uneasy surmise as Mrs. Whitehead appeared in the doorway, her pale blue morning gown flowing around her as if she were gliding rather than walking.

"Good morning, girls. Bridget, dear, I have a blouse here that needs some attention. Do you mind taking care of it after breakfast? And Nora, before you leave, I'll need you to fetch a few things from the market. The butcher's been terribly unreliable lately, and I want to be sure we're prepared for the dinner party Saturday night."

"Yes, ma'am," Nora replied with a quick curtsy, her accent still thick with the melodic timbre of her homeland, though somewhat modulated by six months' immersion in Gotham's dialectal influence.

"And be sure to see Mr. Whitehead about your wages before he leaves for the office."

"Yes, ma'am." The girls looked at each other, Bridget noting a desperate pleading in Nora's eyes.

"Excuse me, ma'am," Bridget spoke up, "but I don't mind going to market today. Nora can do the blouse if you don't mind. She works very well at her needle. Much better than me, I assure you."

"As you wish, dear. Here, Nora," handing her the blouse with a curt nod before disappearing into the home's private apartments.

"I could see it would only take a minute. Go to it, girl. I'll get the market list from Cook."

"I don't want to be missin' me wages."

"You'll be done in no time at all. Go to't, girl. I'll take care of the clearing and washing-up too. Have fun today," the older girl said with another mischievous wink, "and see you tonight."

Bridget quickly followed Mrs. Whitehead out while Nora put the blouse in a clean, safe spot in the sitting room and proceeded with the sweeping, dusting, making beds, emptying chamber pots and filling the lamps with oil while the family breakfasted. Her day off's morning housemaid work completed, she quickly retrieved the delicate garment and rushed back upstairs as Bridget helped Cook clear and clean.

Indeed, Bridget was right – it only took two or three minutes to complete the task. Nora finished tidying up the sewing room and, returning to her room next door, removed, folded and put away her apron. She then changed into her simple but neat green skirt with a white blouse that still looked fresh despite the wear. Carefully, she fit her vibrant hair under her white straw hat, brushing the tresses that gleamed down her back. Checking herself quickly in the mirror with a final prink, she dropped off the blouse and made her way to the morning room where Mr. Whitehead sat enjoying a post-prandial cigar while reading the newspaper, his round spectacles perched on his nose. He barely glanced up as she entered, his eyes fixed on some intriguing story, possibly, given his interests, one explicating President Roosevelt's latest reform.

"Good morning, Mr. Whitehead," Nora said quietly, standing just inside the door.

He grunted in response, but after a moment, looked up suddenly and smiled. "Come in, my young lass, no standing on ceremony here, you know," he said pleasantly in a playful mock of her Irish lilt.

"Missus says I'm to see you about me wages, sir."

Without another word, he reached into his pocket, pulled out a small leather wallet, and extracted a few crisp notes. He handed them to her, his dark eyes looking over his spectacles directly into her sparkling greens, his smile widening. She looked down, noting, as she always did on these occasions, the size of the hand holding her precious pay, the light downy hair covering the back, spreading to the segments of each finger beyond the knuckles, the trim neatness of the fingernails with their carefully rounded edges. His hands were both powerful and delicate at the same time and so very soft and clean. Their hands touched briefly as the money changed from one to the other, his fingers brushing her palm as he released the bills; then, placing his left hand under hers in the friendliest of gestures, he smiled "All good, Nora?"

"Yes, sir, thank you, sir," she murmured.

Continuing to hold her hand gently in his, he casually continued, "I was wondering, my dear, if there was something you might be able to do for me."

"Today is Nora's day off, Wendell," Mrs. Whitehead said, suddenly appearing at the door. "Don't keep her, please; it isn't fair. Be off, my dear."

With a keen semblance of relief, only partially diminished by Mr. Whitehead's aborted request, Nora felt his swift release of her hand as he returned immediately to his paper. She looked down at the four dollar-bills in her delicate hands, coarsened only slightly by work. It wasn't much by the Whiteheads' standards, certainly, but it was enough – enough for her to purchase a few pleasures and a few treasures, enough to send a portion back home to her family, enough to keep them afloat for another month, enough, perhaps, to bring her sister over in a year or so. She quickly tucked the money into her pocket and brushed past Mrs. Whitehead at the door with a barely breathed, "Thank you, ma'am."

She left the house through the servants' entrance, stepping into the sweet warmth of the summer sun. The air had a way of sticking to you in New York's typical thick and humid summers, but this morning was clement and light. The energy of the city pulsing through the streets added to her excitement as people bustled past her, horse-drawn carriages clattered along the cobblestones, and street vendors called out to passersby. Surrounded by such heavy noise and commotion, she might have been a million miles from her family home in Mullingar.

Nora made her way to the post office, threading through the crowded, filth-ridden streets. The post office was busy, as usual, with people of all sorts queuing up to send letters and packages. She made out her envelope quickly and patiently waited her turn. When she finally reached the counter, she handed the vital missive to the clerk along with her nickel for postage.

"For Ireland," she said softly, her accent momentarily catching the man's attention. He nodded and took the letter, stamping it with a heavy hand before placing it in the pile for overseas mail. That task completed, Nora felt lighter, her duty to her family fulfilled for the week. Now, there was only one more matter of importance – her day with Jack.

Jack Doyle was a handsome young man from Cobh in County Cork, with dark hair and a broad smile. Bridget had introduced them seven or eight Sundays ago at Mass, their shared heritage drawing them together in a city that felt so foreign to them both. He worked on the docks, a job as grueling and grimy as it was dangerous, but he had dreams of something more. They all did, really. They all came to America with dreams.

Nora made her way to the docks where Jack was finishing his shift. She spotted him easily, standing tall among the other men – Polacks and Eyeties mostly, he'd said; Catholic, yes, but a little rough – as they unloaded heavy crates from a ship. His shirt was soiled and soaked with dirt and sweat, the muscles in his arms straining as he worked, giving her a quiet thrill. Catching her slim figure approaching, he smiled jubilantly.

"Nora!" he called out, waving as he jogged over to meet her. "You're early!"

"I've finished for the day," she replied with a grin. "Bridie helped me with the chores. And ye?"

"Aye, just done. Let me clean up, and we can go."

Jack disappeared into the small workers' shed nearby, emerging a few short minutes later, clean and fresh, his hair slicked back and wearing a new, clean shirt.

"Where shall we go today?" Jack asked, slipping his laborer's hand into hers as they strolled along. "I was tinkin' of Coney Island."

"Oooooh, I'd be quare afeard to go near the ferry after what happened yestern, God help them poor souls!"

"Sure, darlin', but the General Slocum was an excursion steamboat, not a ferry. You've nothing to fear, *a chuisle.*"

She smiled at the endearment, but there was no changing her mind, with reports of over a thousand people perishing in the East River still being shouted from every corner newsstand. Choosing instead to simply walk the streets of Lower Manhattan like a pair of wandering rocks, they would see what kind of mischief they could get up to.

The sun cast a golden glow over the bustling streets while the air was thick with the mingling scents of fresh bread from corner bakeries, the briny tang of the nearby river and bay, and the ever-present soot and smoke of coal-fired industry. The streets were alive with noisy activity – vendors shouting their wares in a dozen different tongues, trolley cars clattering over steel rails, the scent of hot iron and oil lingering in their wake, and well-dressed businessmen weaving through the throng of immigrants, factory workers, hawkers and waifs. Amidst the chaos, they walked side by side, their steps desultory but steady.

Jack's flat cap sat neatly atop his dark hair, his face bearing a faint patina of sweat, his posture upright, proud, betraying a quiet determination. Nora's straw hat, adorned with a pale blue ribbon, sat at a slight angle, a jaunty jingle upon her carefully arranged hair, pins at the ready for the occasional masher, though that was something she need not fear when walking with Jack.

Their conversation was lively but not too loud, lost amidst the boisterous sounds of the street. They stopped for a half hour or so at the new nickelodeon, having first purchased some nuts to munch during the show, after which they continued their slow perambulation. Jack glanced at Nora constantly, his bright eyes tinged with an inchoate concern. Perhaps he spoke of the job he hoped to secure at a printing house or as a construction worker on the new subway. Nora listened intently, her lips curving into a bright smile when she responded, her words always quick and confident when she was with him. She, too, had dreams of a position outside of service – perhaps as a seamstress in a garment shop or as a typist in an office. Even just working in an hotel instead of a private home would be a step up, she believed, and he agreed absent-mindedly.

An automobile chugged by raucously, a reminder of the ever-changing face of Lower Manhattan, a world in a constant, frenzied motion. But for this young man and woman, on this warm June evening, the city seemed perfectly still, poised on the edge of infinite possibilities.

"Where shall we dine tonight, my lovely?"

"Well, sir, since you're offerin', I would say Delmonico's."

"Delmonico's it is, milady! Let me call for my chariot!"

They laughed together while walking past the Jewish and Italian delicatessens, finally settling on a modest oyster bar in the Bowery where they sat on stools and together finished several dozen oysters with brown bread and tea.

"Sure, an't it grand now and then to be doin' nothin' at all, just to take in the city? Don't ye tink so yourself?"

"Yis, as long as it's with you, Nora darlin'."

As the evening meal concluded, however, Nora's face was clouded with the suspicion that Jack had something serious – even unpleasant perhaps – on his mind. She threw out a few prompts, but if he saw the hook, he certainly wasn't biting. Finally, she asked him to just come out with it – if it was something he needed to say, then he should just say it.

"I'm going home, Nora. Me Mum is sick. I got a telegram from me Da two days ago. 'Mother dying. Come home.' That's all it said. Sure, I'm leavin' Saturday."

"I'm so sorry, Jack, truly. Did ye know she was ailin'?"

"Nah, not really. He mentioned in his last letter that she was poorly, but not this. Nothin' like this."

In the long pause, he paid for dinner, and they quietly left the bar, walking into the darkling city. Pensive and a touch forlorn now, they continued their slow meander, breaking the silence after a while to note the evening's final light reflected on the white marble arch of Washington Square. By custom, at nightfall, they walked to Astor Place, where there was a dark, quiet corner where they could cuddle and kiss. There was a more somber, almost desperate quality this evening, tinged with a greater urgency than she had ever felt from him before. She often took breaks during their intimacies, more to cool his ardor than to catch her breath, but this time, she took only one to ask when he would return.

"I don't know, really."

"But you *are* coming back, Jack, aren't ye?"

"My life is here now, Nora. Me Da knows this. I'm an American now, just like you. Not citizens yet, maybe, but we're both Americans now, an't we? Nah, I'll be back. And I'll be back for you, Nora. You know how I feel about you. You know that... well, in time..."

The only answer to this was the one Bridget had been preparing her for. As they resumed, it was now she who pressed against him. Abandoning her practice of preventing his hands from roaming where they oughtn't, she now moved them herself from her waist up to where she had always stopped them from resting before. Nervously, she unbuttoned his trousers and slipped her hands in and down. Though well prepared by her roommate for what she'd find and what to do, it still came as a bit of a shock, but recollecting clearly all she had been told and shown, she began the slow movement Bridget had demonstrated for her. His hands became more urgent, but she did nothing to dissuade, increasing her pace, sensing her own power as she did. He stopped kissing her and, leaning in, allowed her ear, neck, and hair to absorb his moans in the cooling June night air, exciting her now as well, and, without thinking, relying entirely on her own instincts, she brought him to the final moment. He gave a quiet cry, and she joined him, taken aback, despite her foreknowledge, by his release into her tender hands.

They readjusted themselves before emerging from the doorway and continued in a profound silence until they reached the spot where they typically parted on their Thursdays together. She preferred walking the last few blocks on her own.

"You'll remember me now, Jack, won't ye?"

"You know you've had my heart for many weeks now, Nora. I'll come back to you. I promise."

Checking that all the doors and windows were secure and putting out the one lamp left on in the drawing room, Nora climbed the four flights of stairs quietly. Quickly and quietly, she changed into her sleeping shift and clambered into the plain, iron-frame bed. She and Bridget often stayed up later than they should, given their long days of hard work, talking into the night in close whispers. Typically, it was Bridget who controlled the conversation – she who was older and more seasoned, being so much longer a guest in the United States, and with an American fellah to boot. Bridget proudly shared her knowledge and experience, but tonight was Nora's night to share, and Bridget enjoyed the story so much she asked Nora to tell it all again, this time slowly, while she listened, cooing and purring in a quiet flutter.

The talking having ceased, and with Bridget's gentle snore in the background, Nora played the scene again in her head – of Jack's hands on her breasts, his breath on her cheek, his groans in her ear, and of her hands taking control – as she reached down to lift her nightgown, quickly moving her practiced fingers, thinking again of everything, all blurry and delicious now, merging in her teeming brain with the large, strong, capable, hirsute hands of Mr. Wendell Whitehead holding hers, until she too released into the hands of a deep and quiet slumber, that priceless recharge so necessary to abide another day of work.

Success Story

today

You would be forgiven for thinking, given the expression on his face, that he was looking at a serpent, camouflaged in his private Eden but coiled, ready to strike, as the glow from the document illuminated his visage in the room's dim light. His eyes skimmed over it like a stone tossed from a marly shore, skipping freely, no longer taking in the words as he had no reason to pierce the meaning of the arcane phrases of the factitious legal kludge shining before him in the darkness. The forensic phraseology had already been explicated to him in plain language, understandable even by the limited resources of his mental acumen, a handicap that attenuated his rise for many years. It was only in the sixth decade of his existence that the various strands of his extensive and disparate life experiences twined together into a rope strong enough to pull himself up, along with his entire family, which had always been his prime motivation, at least since he and Lydia first met. True, he never promised her a rose garden, as, in the early days of their marriage, he was wont to say in his homely way, but once the little plot on which they'd staked their all began to flourish, roses were but one of the plentiful varieties of flora to grace the hothouse of their wealth.

Just as the early days were marked by privation and struggle, so his latter life was filled with luxury and success. Perhaps you observed him, working all day in his office, an activity many of his ilk found a drudge, but for Hilbert Osmolovsky, the moving from desk to desk and taking calls from the field, to cajole, to facilitate, to encourage and to reward each triumph were quotidian pleasantries he imbibed like an intoxicant. Perhaps you were able to overhear him as he related his triumphs to his wife and child, a vespertine activity he relished, even though such pleasures paled in comparison to the vainglory of those semi-annual sales meetings where he stood center stage, alone and triumphant, a sequoia amongst mere shoots, reading out the numbers, projecting graphs on screens, laying out future sales and marketing campaigns to the cheers of excited distributors, affiliates, associates, consultants, and brand managers assembled in the auditorium. Or maybe you were present at the convention he organized after the company had reached that significant sales goal, when he displayed their success with so many zeros that it might have been better expressed in scientific notation, an emotional rush to match the professional heights he had attained, primarily through the sheer force of personality – "painting pictures with words" in his wife's colorful phrase – to get an amphitheater amassed with his ship's full complement, springing to their feet, leaping into the air and clutching at the thousands of hundred-dollar bills he threw to them from the stage in flamboyant congratulations and appreciation.

It is true that even amongst this rarefied group, a group considered friends, fellow crewmates, and welcomed allies in the battle of the marketplace, there were dissenting voices, or at least voices that vented frustration in the form of bitter contempt for the products and services they themselves duly signed on to promote. You might know for certain, if you were among those who lived forever on the bottom rungs of the sales organization, working hard and gathering crumbs while fellow toilers earned diamond watches and ruby bracelets on top of the vast sums of commissions paid out for selling wares of questionable authority, whether or not it was one of them who troubled the waters with their displeasure. But Hilbert was unaware of any unhappiness, as he was more than willing to share the bounty of their journey together, much of which was distributed at the capstan of the sales meetings, as it seemed the company possessed letters of marque, given its vast quantity of spoils. Still, even as he created millionaires by the score, admittedly floating on a sea of dejected failures by the thousand, there was plenty left for the Osmolovsky family to fund the homes, the cars, the vacations by private jet, the lavish soirees and the far more brilliant luster he shed upon his wife and child, the joy of which frequently exceeding the elation of standing before the thousands who brought him such wealth. Were you in the extensive throng who felt that more of the bounty needed to be shared, joining in their cacophonous vilifications of fiscal turpitude? Such low murmurings, which Hilbert at first considered adiaphorous, involved a sinuosity of accusation whose invidious power was seemingly the inducement of the wave of wrath exhibited by the authorities whose ferocity he perceived as a tangle of weeds choking out the beauty of his nursery. The dark, quiet of his study was the perfect place to reflect, in the turbid watches of the night, on the bright lights, loud music, and clamorous applause of the latest gathering of the peddlers of dreams he had assembled single-handedly, as he dealt with his current predicament, mostly by avoiding any contemplation of it.

Clashing with authorities is very much a young man's game and one in which he had indulged in his time, the excitement of which, in callow ignorance, was accepted as a pleasant diversion despite the outcome of reprimand, forfeiture, and dependence that such outlandish behavior engendered, for in youth, nothing has great value, or at least no greater value than the thrill and the desire for more thrills.

"When are you going to straighten up and fly right?" his father would cajole after each escapade. "How do you expect to succeed in this world if you keep goofing off?"

But it was not, at least to his mind, goofing off so much as letting off steam, as, like many of you, he did work hard, holding two jobs in addition to attending community college, from which he never quite seemed to graduate, despite apparently applying himself assiduously to his studies. But between flipping burgers during the day and tending bar at night, the toll on schoolwork was not incomprehensible, even if the vision was beyond that of a twenty-year-old flipperty-gibbet, especially when the burger-flipping gave way quickly to being an order-taker and from thence to managing the franchise, certainly some sign of success, or at least that success was not out of reach of this good-natured goof who did not seem to know the proper direction to fly.

It was also as manager that he hired Lydia, for whom he had fallen deeply and sincerely during the job interview and with whom he always managed to schedule time at the restaurant, and afterwards, in the parking lot, as he had, at that point, still not managed sufficient funds to acquire a place of his own. Whether or not they would have married had she not found herself with child is a question that each of them answered differently at different times in their life together, hers being primarily in the negative, especially early on, whilst his, except on one or two occasions, supremely positive, and trying to ensure that her answer matched his more frequently was a major motivation for his pursuing ever greater heights of wealth and fame, even as the air thinned and his vertigo erupted from the dizzying summit to which he had finally climbed.

As Hilbert matured in his marriage, he had had neither a particle of arrogance nor a particle of vanity but seemed content in merely eschewing all unremunerative endeavors by simply grueling out a decent wage to maintain a domicile and to recreate in the evenings with his family, as his father had done. But such a homey predilection for these simple evening pleasures hid a capacious desire for opulence and splendor, which inspired him to grasp at any opportunity, while no prevision could illuminate the sorrow that would attend the joy, although the excitement and pleasure seemed to outweigh the pain and inconvenience of the justified award.

Their financial struggles, which predated their establishment of a home together, continued after the boy was born and even out of diapers and starting school, as Hilbert moved from job to job, the reasons for his dismissal or resignation (the former more often than the latter) varying from instance to instance. It was from the precariousness of their finances that Lydia was taken with the idea of selling the Jayne Fields line of costume jewelry, clothing, and skincare, the commissions for which promised to repay the cost of the startup kit and bring rich rewards beyond. But Lydia struggled to simply win back her initial investment just at a time when Hilbert, looking about for some new place he could earn his bread with the sweat of his brow, accompanied her one evening to a sales party and became taken with the business model Ms. Fields and other like entrepreneurs had chosen to hawk their wares.

He soon learned that the selling of the products did not earn as much in commission as securing hostesses for the parties and, providing even greater remuneration, selling other startup kits. The entire concept of this form of sales and marketing spoke to something deep inside him, as if a bell had rung, and he began to salivate without any knowledge of why. And so, securing a few products to sell, with an understanding that this selection would expand in time, he imitated their compensation system and initiated his sales force by pinching Lydia's colleagues.

Hilbert did not like contemplating the early days, the assistance he received from his wife, the queasy feeling of failure looming, and success always just out of reach. But once he had abandoned the selling of physical items and concentrated wholly on services and non-corporeal products like insurance, the enterprise took off, and its vertiginous ascent over a mere four or five years was the time he most enjoyed reflecting on. But casting off from the world of managing inventory brought him into waters of which he had no knowledge nor instinct for navigating, and the ship seemed to founder even as it gained speed from the increasing vehemence of the trade winds.

You certainly knew he had been warned. His Sales Director was clear that the latest move into financial instruments was highly fraught and one for which the company did not have the proper infrastructure. But the move from product to service to finance was ineluctable once a critical mass had been reached, and suppliers began to seemingly spring from the ground or descend from a machine to request that he implement his forty-thousand-strong sales force to push their products. Their appeals were powerful and fell upon his moist, loamy moral surface like seeds of mixed species, some likely to bloom into radiant splendor, but a few – and it only takes a few – proliferating as choking weeds.

"It's a big enough issue that your reps are referring to the life insurance policy as 'submarine insurance,'" Bob had told him, "But if you add the debit card and loan protection, we're in a new court altogether."

Hilbert, who had played many different games on many different court surfaces, was prepared to take the plunge into any sport likely to be lucrative. Perhaps you were among the force who were not happy – not everyone was cut out for this kind of work, and the only way they would know was by trying – but the idea that the life insurance policies the company represented paid out only if the policyholder "died in a submarine on a Tuesday in August if it is snowing" was an exaggeration that stung rather deeply when brought to his attention. But the new court held a promise of financial products of real value, like payday advances and reverse mortgages, which all could be proud to sell. Sadly, such instruments are designed to be played only by true maestros who understand the stops and frets of such complexities. Sadly, the pitfalls of missteps held much more serious consequences than the succession of returns of the skin creams that turned brown or the clothes whose seams gave out easily from which he had quit. Sadly, he had neither the skill nor talent for reckoning a position when loaded with the ballast of unpaid loans and repossessed properties from which his glorious ship was about to capsize or run aground.

Lydia, originally part of the growing empire in the early days, working the phones and, later, managing the office staff, at least until she was able to step down to a life of shopping and lunching at the club, by this time was distanced enough from the enterprise that hiding the issues was not a difficulty, but their son, Kevin, who was at this point employed in the marketing department, had his mother's ear. He wasn't truly cognizant of the implications of taking on the newest product, as he was trying to develop, on his own, an identity protection package that could be added to the sales bag, as it were, but which, his intellectual prowess not quite measuring up to even the limited means of his father's, was not coming to fruition. Still, his only real purpose at the company was to be prepared to succeed the old man, who, you could see, although not quite ready to retire, was certainly beginning to wilt and wither. Besides, he had made enough to enjoy the well-earned rest and relaxation that was due him, and Kevin was looking forward keenly to his father stepping away and his taking the helm. It was, therefore, certainly a shock to the young man when it was explained to him the true lay of the land and the nature and power of the invading forces gathering at the gates, ready to convert their entire fertile field of dreams to tillage. Hilbert extracted from his progeny the promise that he would refrain from running to his mother, thus allowing him the opportunity to relate the bad news to his wife personally.

His inability to perform that delicate, troublesome task was, he realized, a major factor in his decision. Even as he prepared himself for the final act of becoming signatory to an ingenious, though highly risky, subterfuge, he pondered what would happen if he chose to decline the spurious solution. After all they had done together – putting shoulders to the plough, side by side, as the company was being built – to be shut out of the critical decisions that brought about the downfall, to enjoy the fruits of their labor only to have them whisked away at the eleventh hour, to explain the process of the gargantuan loss and its effect on their future together, this was not a conversation even you would find easy to have with your spouse. And so it was that he conceived, in the last minute, this exit which could facilitate a tolerable resolution.

"Look, Hildy," his attorney responded to his plea for a lifeline, "I told you before. You attracted top reps by offering more in commissions than they actually earn. It doesn't matter how many more you bring on or how many new services you add, you have structured the thing basically like a Ponzi Scheme, and those always have their moment of crashing. That moment is coming whether you like it or not. I will prepare an appropriate document that will keep you out of jail, but not much more than that. How much cash can you raise? Quickly?"

And so there it was in front of him, ready to be executed, his success, once a towering sycamore, now a downed and rotting log to be slipped into the ocean where it would decompose and be distributed throughout the world in microbits of assets – small beer and chump change, where once vintage champagne flowed, and hundred-dollar bills floated on billows. Typing in his signature and returning the document, he reflected ruefully, far from solving his problems, merely shifted them to another forum, while the major issue of informing Lydia would still be on the agenda. It was not a story he relished relating and, as such, it was not likely to enhance his matrimonial situation or bring any reasonable success to his endeavors.

Staring through, rather than at, the document, his mind raced over the decades of labor, trying to discern the whole from the fragments, feeling it unfurl as a succession of triumphs in the financial sector, the speeches, the news articles, the invitations to circles that once excluded him and others like him, to be not just tolerated but admired for his success, he feared now would turn into ignominy and destitution. He had built not just a company but an institution, a verdant empire, an edifice to leave behind that would be a testament to his hard work and infallible discernment. Instead, he is as you see him now, broken and desolate, sitting in his sunless office, seemingly just passing time on a tiny plot of land, rank and gross, a fetid tract of broken promises, aground, wrecked and ruined, with a simple future of nothing but dust.

Last Rights

tomorrow

<u>"I'm back!"</u>

The meetroom was full and suffused with the susurration of various individual colloquies when it went suddenly silent as Chance Whittaker shimmered in. After that brief, quiet moment, with all eyes turned to her, the gathering spontaneously erupted into a raucous snapplause.

"I'm back!" Chance cried with a sheepish smile as the snapping subsided. "It was no biggie, y'know. Just a touch of cancer."

"Hey, cancer's nothing to be glib about. People used to die from that smacky."

"Pancreas, but not very far along, righty."

"Still. Happy to have you back."

"Thanky!"

"Wall, Ah thank we can begin," Sloane Vanderbliss, the pool leader, drawled. "Since Chance is back with us, let's start with the data centers. Ah know you never left your post during recovery –"

"Two days in Bowash."

"Wall, we won't count that. You've been monitorin' your data center throughout, righty? Let's hear 'bout that."

Chance then provided the update on the center she managed up in Peawanuk, showing the energy inputs, fluctuations, recissions and frequency of data keyups. She was followed by Recip Juanez and Quandun Mercy, the only other two Security Pool members who also managed data centers. Sloane continued with the next agenda item: aibot security.

"How's the aibot incursion in the squib flow, Facil?"

"Under control. Lucy and Jen are on de flutters and Fred recused de food variant last week. Just a blippy. All's back."

"So much for the price of eggs, eh?" quipped Maris Pelletier.

"Four quan to the dozen," someone else quipped in response, provoking a round of muted laughter.

"Enough. Shoozy shoozy, please. Facil, could you invoke Fred, please?"

"Sure ting," Facil responded equably as he moved his hand horizontally, and the image of the Aibot Fred materialized. He had a smooth, angelic, though wooden, face, young, handsome, but, like all aibots, lacking surface details of a human: no lines, no pores, no facial hair, presenting an almost plastic appearance.

"Aibot 345 reporting," he said in his flat affect.

"This is Sloane Vanderbliss, Chair of the Westron Fiscalnet Security Pool. Please explain the price blip of sector B95/7."

The aibot provided a series of numbers, matrices, and tangents to justify the momentary blip and then explained the tracing and treatment programs that were run to analyze and correct the keyups.

"What are the probabilities of a recurrence in the near future?"

"Within the next year, approximately 0.0132% probability of a minor flutter; less than 0.0001% probability of a major turbulence."

"Thanky, Fred. Release." And with that dismissal, Aibot 345 dissolved without a word.

And so, the meeting ground on as each pool member reported and every topic was fully covered until the final agenda item, the delegation from Africa.

"Most are going to Essay, but we're gettin' a significant contingent here. Again, most will be with the techs, the pols, and the econs, but we have one individual visitin' us. Her name is Verena Chidozie and after her meetin' with Minister Sosha, she'll be stoppin' with Facil, then Farin, then Chance, and finishing up with me, your intrepy leader. So, the four of us'll handle it while, true, the rest of y'all are off easily, though she may choose to vid any o' y'all, so be to the ready."

"Is there really any chance of a hookup?"

"Integration," Sloane corrected him; "That's up to the pols."

"True, but seriously. We're security. If we say they're not ready, we can kibosh them, can't we?"

"Ah'd like to think they'd listen to us, but, no, final word's with the pols. Listen. Do your jobs. This Chidozie has full digital clearance. Remember, they're only sendin' one to the Security Pool, so they know how sensitive this all is. Full cooperation, y'all. Am I clear?"

The committee responded with a full snapplause, and everyone around Chance dissolved as the meetroom changed back into her office. She stared at the empty space for a brief moment or two, stretched, and then called for her workstation.

Central Casting

The briefing was held in a hangar near a secret runway just outside Mandela, South Africa. As Verena Chidozie entered, she counted at least one hundred people gathered there, with more arriving. They were arranged in the groups in which they would be working, but Verena noted that the groupings also seemed to follow tribal association and even skin hue to a certain extent, with the primarily jet black politicos from the south in the front rows while the northern, tawnier tribes, which formed the bulk of the economics, science, and digital teams, were sitting behind them. Verena chose to stand alone at the back of the hangar.

First Minister Queen M'becki began things with a review of the process over the past twenty years. She spoke of the decision of her predecessor to attempt integration with the worldnet, of the delegation that failed nearly a decade ago, of the committee meetings in Eastron that had met with notable success, of the stormy conferences with the members of the Westron Commissionats, and finally of the mission ahead of them.

"You be vanguard to a new era, one that will finally link PanAfrica to rest of world. I know there be elements prefer we continue our own course alone. I understand these positions. Their arguments for continued segregation be strong. Yes, there be difficult adjustments if we move forward. Many rights we hold dear will be modified. Not lost, as some say, but, yes, modified. But it be will of African peoples to move beyond isolation, to taste benefits of goods, services, and technologies that Northern World developed.

"There be difficult days ahead. Agreement to integration not be a given. Indeed, our own representatives intimated there be strong opposition in Westron especially. Your mission be not simply to gather data in chosen areas of your expertise, but to act as ambassadors to Northern World. For millennia, northern peoples looked to our continent for people to enslave, to conquer, to exploit… or to ignore. Finally, now we see strong consensus there to welcome us as equal partners. But let us never forget there also be strong minority element that does not, and it be that element *we* must conquer. But if we do, and integration be way forward, the future of PanAfrica be bright!"

There was more encouragement, and then ViceGeneral Kgosi Uhuto presented the logistics of travel and the various assignments, while SubChair Induna Oporto handed out the briefs. Verena took her brief without looking at the subchair and retreated to her barracks to review, pack, and prepare for transport. She – and she alone – traveled without consort, dealing, as she would be, with sensitive security issues. Her first stop, with most of the committee groups, was in Grain-Iowa to meet with Ennay's First Minister, then on by herself to Socal to work with someone named Facil Ryzhov. Every stop provided ample sightseeing opportunities, which she always enjoyed on assignments abroad, except the data center in the far north. She was not looking forward to *that* trip in the middle of winter.

A Day in the Life

"Good morning, Chance."

It was never Chance's habit to address aibots conversationally, even those programmed with that capability. So, rather than respond, she simply rose from her bed and attended to her morning routine. The aibot continued to address her, quite used to her ways.

"Your cuppajay is ready. Which breakfast would you like this morning?"

"Number three."

"It will be ready in twenty minutes. Instigating morning feed to your shower."

Chance enjoyed catching up on news while showering. The aibot would bring up her comms while she ate her breakfast. Once completed, she called for her day's agenda, transformed her kitchen into her workstation, and began the task of running through the latest data, analyzing the keyups, and determining any need for coding. This morning her comm pinged early. It was Sloane. What in hellsy could *he* want so early?

"Just checking in."

"Thanky, Moosey."

"Shoozy shoozy. Truly, though. Are you through the backlog?'

"Nearly. I was going to breaky soon and check out the data center before lunch."

"Wall, anythin' of interest?"

"I noticed a number of weep flutters in the price vols. They seem to have come from Facil's district."

"All in the last two days?"

"True, how d'ya know?"

"Our African friend is with him, so Ah assume he's showin' her things. Nothin' permanent?"

"Nopey. Just flutters."

"Wall, put a bot on it and see what turns up."

"Already done."

"Take it easily, my girl."

"Thanky, Moosey."

"Byebye, Booby."

Sloane cut the communication after returning Chance's smile at their friendly, private sobriquets. After a few more inputs, she entered the covert, opened the case with the envirosuits and put one on, carefully attaching the helmet, connecting the oxygen supply. She did not activate the heating element as she would not be going outdoors. With that, she opened the airlock and headed into the data center.

The data center was a separate building, connected to her living quarters by a causeway. The temperature control ended at the door, but at least the causeway was enclosed, preventing the buffeting of the wind and the blinding of the snow, and allowing the heat to flow through the ceiling ducts from the data center to her domicile. A quick temp check showed it to be nearing negative forty outside. About normal for that time of year.

The heat from the data cores, despite the energy drainoff for her domicile, still kept the center quite a bit warmer than the outside world, though hardly balmy enough to remove the suit but just mild enough that she could take off the helmet if she wanted to. She didn't want to. She walked from core to core with her padd, checking each readout and external frame. She saw a minor issue on Core 178 and called Aibot 23 to investigate. Aibot 23 emanated as female and also went by the name Mandy, though she was well aware that Chance, unlike most others, preferred using numbers than names and therefore identified herself with her numerical designation.

It took well over an hour working with Aibot 23 to readjust the tau lepton flows, and Chance was hot enough that she contemplated removing her helmet but chose instead to perspire a little. Once the job was completed, she released the bot, returned through the causeway, disrobed, and sat down to a short, small midday meal, during which Aibot 12 announced, "Your staples are arriving." She waited until she had completed the meal and sent the kitchenware to the wash before going into the portcullis of her entrance to retrieve and put away the groceries and other items which had been delivered by autocar.

The afternoon work was always on the light side and completed early enough for Chance to exercise in the workout area and then lie under the UV lamps for an hour. She finished the workday by reading comms, sending some herself, doing a final diagnostic, and relaxing with her evening feeds before dinner. After dinner, she typically listened quietly to some relaxing music or watched an old vid of her and Sfreena, which sometimes relaxed her but, more often than not, brought on a mild, cathartic crying jag, as it did this evening. Prior to bedtime, she would choose between a drowse program, a mild soporific, or pleasuring herself to sleep. This evening, she chose all three.

Ayati

"If you tink I'm happy for you, well, I'm not, *yene mare.* Dey bad people dere."

"This is not my first time over there, *Ayati.* You remember, do you not?"

"Yes, I remember, and I remember what happened when your Aba and Ema went."

"That was long ago, *Ayati*."

"Dey don't change, de whites."

After Verena had been tapped to join the new delegation, she knew it would be difficult telling her grandmother. She had opposed every trip she made since her parents were killed in Westron nearly thirty years before.

"I am going to Ennay, not Eeyoo, anyway."

"Don't know de stupid names."

Verena smiled to herself as she moved around her grandmother's kitchen, tidying up, more to keep busy and avoid looking her grandmother in the eye than anything requiring her assistance. Her grandmother was old, but not so old that she couldn't look after herself.

"Yes, *Ayati*: I am going to America, northern sector, not Europa."

"Europe!"

"Yes, Europe. Where Momsa and Pomsa went. I know. Not going there."

"Dey all white. Can't trust dem. Dey have no rights dere, yes? No freedoms! No privacy! No *rights*! Dangerous dere, *yene mare*."

"You know the work I do, *Ayati*. It can be dangerous. But you did raise a very tough granddaughter, *Ayati*."

"Your parents tough too. Look what happened. No, dey destroyed de world, dey did. De War. De Disruption, dey call it. Dey did it! Remember dat!"

Verena chose to forego reminding her grandmother the major role the Asian nations had in the War and the subsequent Disruption. She had neither the time nor the inclination to enter that discussion again.

"I will be very careful, *Ayati*. I promise."

"You come home to me, *yene mare*. You come home to Africa. Where's it safe."

<u>Verena at the Fa's</u>

Because they were both in same pool and because both their names began with "Fa", they were, of course, in the humor of the time, referred to as "the Fa's," the joke being that "Fazzy" was slang for "Fathead," so a joke neither one particularly cared for. Facil's setup was close by a boutique hotel, which suited both Verena and Facil nicely, as the latter did not suffer guests well, and the former preferred not to invade a bachelor establishment.

That the two took an instant dislike to each other was also unsurprising given their backgrounds and proclivities. As a result, the first two days were quite chilly despite the pleasant break in the winter clime. The instruction to be as cooperative as possible notwithstanding, Facil, who shared the skepticism of many others in the pool regarding the advisability of this second attempt at integration, chose to respond to Verena's questions with the minimum number of syllables possible while refraining from volunteering any additional information. He was also extremely condescending, which Verena expected and knew precisely how to handle. She allowed him to explain the basics of the various nets, with their nodes and matrices and lepton flutters, keeping hidden her highly advanced knowledge of coding, aibot coherence, and quantum dynamics.

After those first two days, once Verena had understood how the clusters and the dineurons of the subjunctive programs worked, and she was able to follow Aibot Jane and Aibot Fred through the junctions of the fiscalnet with the commnet and restnet, her attitude underwent a dramatic change, as she seemed to suddenly warm to the older man, with his funny ticks, odd accent, and strange moods. On the third day, therefore, instead of heading back to her hotel or visiting more local attractions, she asked if he would care to dine with her that evening. He declined twice, but as she pressed him, he could hardly continue to refuse. He knew a small place nearby with a limited menu but was cozy and pleasant. He rarely dined out, but when he did, it was typically at the Negro Corazon Coapa bistro. After the first two courses and beginning the second bottle of wine, Facil became more expansive, although no less bristly.

"My parents grew up in Eeyoo. Zey had it ze verst, y'know. I remember ze stories my Pappy used to tell – my grandfather, that is – about ze earlies. I can still see him vis his radiation scars on his face. It vas a terrible ting, ze Var."

"I have been to Eeyoo. Paris most recently. Even today, it is not half of what you have here."

"You been to Eastron too, I hear. Vat is zat like?"

"China is nice. In places. The rest…" she ended with a shrug. "But tell me how you settled here."

So, he told her of the long migration of his grandparents and parents, coming even before the great Westron unification, moving from city to city to find work, finally settling in the southwest portion of Ennay, which had taken the least amount of damage in the north.

"It vas before ze residency visas, ven you could live anyvere. My father vas in construction, a booming business fifty years ago. But I knew I vanted to get digital. I love ze bots – ai and ro – and now I enjoy verking vis zem more zan people, actually. True!" And with that, Facil gave a great laugh.

This was Verena's first journey to Westron in several years, and the use of bots had increased exponentially since then. She noted how some people treated them like humans, preferring to use their names to their number designations. Facil seemed particularly attached to his bots. He even had two robots in his domicile where most people had only one. "One for day and one for night," he joked, but looking at Wendy, the nighttime bot, Verena thought perhaps it wasn't such a joke and felt rather creepy about the whole thing.

Of course, she was unused to having robots roaming around her home back in Mandela. But she kept such thoughts to herself as she continued to ask pertinent questions with a disarming smile. She had spent the day glancing at the fiscalnet only tangentially while seeming to concentrate on the nexus between the commnet and the Ennay intranet, which Facil watched carefully. She felt claustrophobic all day with his constant hovering and thought the evening would loosen things up a bit, and, indeed, the more wine consumed, the more she learned, easing the rest of the time she had to spend there and making her overall stay with Facil extraordinarily illuminating.

Her stay in Wayne-Nebraska was also just a week, but she and Farin hit it off immediately. Farin's wife, Mowena, and their two children were also welcoming and delightful, the evening meals filled with laughter without any gloomy references to the past. During the day, Farin was extremely helpful, not just answering questions but anticipating what

Verena would be most interested in, opening each program, routine, and subroutine that he thought she would find of value. He even turned Aibot Norman over for her exclusive use if she wanted it.

"I'm very lucky to get this job, yeah," he mentioned during one of their breaks. "Security alone is rather high in the pool pantheon, but specifically for the fiscalnet? Yeah, that's a big honor. Big honor, truly. It's how we can afford the visa for this house!" he laughed. "But I am very proud of the work I do. Ensuring price stability and secure management of one's assets, yeah; that's critically important to every citizen of Westron. Eastron, too, I imagine, although you'd know more about that than I. Only Sloane deals with our counterparts over there, but he reports to us and, yeah, keeps us updated. The amount of checking and double-checking – by us and the aibots – is quite astounding, if you consider it. Truly booly, yeah."

"What do you mean?"

And so Farin took her step by step through how the fiscalnet ensured price stability, by continually assessing costs throughout the sourcing, production, and transportation processes, arranging for enough people for necessary services, managing projected demand, and ensuring that pricing – regardless of the source of the commodity or service – is so transparent that it becomes intractable, thus eliminating price fluctuations, inflation or any other disruptive element in the economy. Farin's job had to do specifically with securing the numerous safecaches for every citizen in Westron. Facil dealt more with price controls, Sloane with incursions and quan balancing, Recip with nodes and connectors ("It's really too bad you're not visiting Recip – she's terrific"), Fessle with the quantum variances, and on and on, the only person she visited that actually explained what each of the twentyseven members of the Security Pool did.

"But ensuring such transparency and stability requires serious incursion into people's lives. We know you no longer have right to privacy and even some of what we would consider basic rights, as in speech and some choices. Is that not a problem for you?"

"True, for some maybe, but no not really for me. I mean, we don't talk much about the War and the Disruption, yeah, it doesn't really do good to dwell on the past, but, yeah, I think the obsession over privacy and religion was the main cause for all of that smacky."

"I thought it was greed."

"True, there's always been greed, yeah, human nature, righty? But it never led to anything like the Disruption! I think if you asked most people in Westron whether they prefer the old rights or the peace and prosperity of today, yeah, they would choose what we've got now, yeah, easypeasy."

By the time she left Nebraska, she and the young man were good friends, with Rowena's promise to vid her regularly and the girls calling her "Auntie Vreenie." She was not looking forward to a week in the frozen north, especially as she had everything she needed by this time, but it was her last stop but one, and she still had her main job to complete.

On Her Majesty's Secret Service

She wasn't terribly surprised she had been tapped for the assignment. She was, after all, one of the few in Africa who had visited Eastron and was also part of the last Westron mission. In fact, she'd been nearly everywhere, Eeyoo, Ennay, Essay, China, Japan, and even spots in Oceanesia. She was a firstclass coder and a highly diplomatic pol. Not to mention the perfect spy. But she was a little old for the assignment – over forty whilst all the others were in their thirties and some even their twenties. They were from all over the continent, although most from the south. Living in Mandela, she was also close to the powerbrokers but preferred working behind the scenes. Her life was structured and ascetic but with a few simple luxuries like her getaway in the Serengeti. Few in Africa could afford an apartment in Mandela and a home – no matter how small and rustic – elsewhere. She was a loner and liked it that way, taking love and friendship in occasional small bites. Born in the Horn, raised in the Sahel, working in the south, Verena Chidozie was a child of Africa and fiercely devoted to her parent.

A week prior to the big briefing outside Mandela, about two days after receiving notice that she would be part of the expedition, she had been called into SubMinister Butho G'Wanni's office. She knew the subminister somewhat, although she had never worked for him directly before. She knew him well enough to know that "SubMinister of Ancient Culture" was a title that hid his true position. They were both, after all, secretly assigned to a different agency altogether.

"You were surprised at the assignment, Agent Chidozie?" he began, looking intensely at Verena.

"A little, yes, SubMinister. I assume from being called here in the middle of the night that the assignment is more than checking out their security nets."

"More than, yes, but not instead of. You will be assigned the security team in charge of the fiscalnet, their entire finance system, as you know. You will do that job as assigned, is that understood, Agent Chidozie?"

"Yes, SubMinister. But in addition…?"

"Yes, in addition, I want you to run diagnostics on the other nets as well. If you get caught, don't worry. In fact, it might help if you did get caught, as nosing about will be your fallback cover. Your real job is to scuttle the deal."

Trained as she had been to hide her emotions, Verena could not help but betray surprise at this.

"Yes, Agent Chidozie? You seem to have a question."

"Apologies, SubMinister--"

"Between us and within these walls, you may call me by my true title, Agent Chidozie."

"Yes, General. I was wondering, first, how you expect me to do this, and, well, perhaps I do not have a right to ask, but…"

"Why?"

"Yes, General. Why?"

"Because our political leaders want this too much. They are desperate and desperate people make mistakes. It is true that Africa had been mostly left out of the Great War and subsequent – what do they call it? 'Disruption'? A nice euphemism, that! More like 'Destruction'. Or 'Disintegration', eh, Agent Chidozie?

Verena correctly surmised that that was a rhetorical question and remained silent, waiting for the coin – or quan – to drop.

"So it is that we mostly had time to catch up to the rest of the world as they descended into their own heart of darkness. But it wasn't long – within a few decades really – that they, especially the west, picked up pace and surpassed us once again. And now our people want all that 'tecky'."

The general practically spat the last word with anger and disdain. Verena chose to continue listening in silence.

"So, now we be moving to new era, neh? We be on verge of integration. Bah!"

Again, Verena maintained a stony silence in the face of the general's mocking of the first minister – his age and status clearly gave him that privilege – but her mind was racing. What was the old man getting at?

"We can make our own tecky. We have brains here enough. I don't trust the whites. I never have, and I never will. Don't tell me they didn't engineer our being kept behind. You know they did! They raped our continent for centuries. Don't tell me they won't do it again once we're all integrated into their systems. They don't believe in the same rights we do. Consider what they do to their own and what that would mean they do to us. No, the future of PanAfrica is not with them. You find this amusing, Agent Chidozie?"

Surprised she had betrayed herself once more in front of the old man, she responded quickly, "No, General!"

"Then why the smile? Explain."

"Apologies, General, it is just that… well, you remind me of my grandmother."

"The one who raised you. The Amhara."

"Yes, General," Verena responded, this time successfully masking her distaste at his reference to her grandmother's tribe and the even greater distaste at the recollection of her father's parents his comment evoked. She always avoided thinking of them if she could.

"She is a wise woman, your grandmother, I think."

Verena had to step carefully here. She knew her grandmother and this general to whom she had been seconded were in the minority, most Africans seeing the richness of life in the North on the news feeds and vids and wanting all those bots and other techs. Verena herself was torn, having seen it up close and experienced some of those luxuries, but her vision was also shaded by the experience of the disastrous attempt ten years earlier, not to mention the murder of her parents two decades before that. The general had made his intentions clear, however, and, while invited to explain her difference of opinion, she knew to be cautious.

"You do not think they have been humbled by the Disruption?"

"Maybe the first generations were, but the current one…? No. Not I. Arrogant! All of them! Scuttle the deal. Find a reason."

"And if I don't?"

"Invent one."

And there it was. That was something new. She had never disobeyed an order before and she was not wont to now, but then she had never been ordered to commit treason before. Sure, gathering data or even planting data, not to mention creating virus incursions, had been her expertise, but it was always performed in furtherance of PanAfrica state policy. The general's prejudice was clearly affecting his judgement, but G'Wanni was her superior. Verena prayed she would find something and not have to deal with the moral dilemma placed before her.

Verena Takes a Chance

"Oh my! Oh my! I haven't laughed like that in such a long time!"

"But it is quite true! Every word of it!"

"Truly, truly, but still …"

And with that, Chance broke out again until tears ran down her face. Verena had been staying with Chance for four days. The first day was rather frosty, and not just because the temperature outside had dropped below negative fifty. Chance's domicile was well insulated and heated thoroughly by the hundreds of data columns in the building next door. Verena had virtually memorized her entire brief on Chance and knew she could be prickly. Practically a hermit after the tragic death of her wife and child during childbirth two years previously, she never even took a vacation from her remote spot in the north, even declining rehab in Bowash during her cancer treatment.

So, the first day had been strictly business, with Chance showing her visitor everything she was supposed to, although she did find it a little odd that Verena's interest in the fiscalnet was greater than the aibots that policed the full worldnet, which she had assumed would be her main concern. It was also a little difficult for the two women to live in close proximity as the domicile was designed for one, and there was obviously no convenient hotel, the transportation hub itself nearly ten miles away and, even by transport, the nearest hotel more than an hour beyond that.

The first night was tricky, but by the evening of the third day, Chance's guard was sufficiently lowered to allow personal stories to be traded back and forth, and the one about Verena's cousins was just too delicious to not laugh. And with that, they were finally getting on like old friends, as Verena had hoped.

The fourth day involved much more work in the data core despite the fact that Verena's main mission was understanding the security aibots. She noticed that Chance used them less than the others did, preferring to do most coding on her own, not to mention having no robots to aid her in manual tasks. Verena followed Chance down the various subatomic corridors of the neural nets, feigning ignorance and amazement at each turn. Chance was slowly warming to her visitor and even secretly wondering if it was time she requested a transfer and spent more time among people again.

Later that evening, after dinner and over a couple of small glasses of minor intoxicants, Verena carefully chose the moment to get political. She knew she had what she needed to complete her assignments, and she knew her final visit with Sloane Vanderbliss was just perfunctory box ticking. She came at it tangentially, putting her muled feet up on the stool in front of her comfochair.

"I notice you refer to the bots by their numbers and not their names, the way the others do. Why is that?"

Perhaps it was the wrong way, given how Chance suddenly tensed.

"Apologies," Verena offered, "am I getting too personal?"

"No, no, that's okee. I don't mind. You can ask me anything. But nopey, it's just that I don't want to think of them as human. They're not. True, they're programmed to talk human and, when they materialize, they look human, sissyso anyway, but they're not, y'know. And I don't want to forget that. I think sometimes people do, despite the fact that they've chosen old, preWar names for them."

"Some have quite personal relationships with them. Or maybe just the robots."

"No, you're righty, the aibots too. I think it's duzzy myself."

"Apologies, I do not know all your slang. 'Duzzy?'"

"Duzzy. Disgusting."

"That is strong."

Chance chose not to respond, pulling her evening gown around her a little tighter.

"As long as we're getting personal here, can I ask *you* a personal question?"

"Certainly, Chance."

"You seem to be quite advanced as a coder. We've been told Africa is far behind us. But you seem…"

"I have been specially trained for this mission," Verena offered cautiously. "That was not terribly personal. May I now get *more* personal?" she asked with a broad smile.

"As long as it isn't 'why do you want to live way out here?' I'm tired of that one."

"No, no, no. I was simply wondering if you wanted this integration or not."

Chance was clearly uncomfortable with this and was struggling for an answer. She had not expected to get into topics outside the nature of her own work and was not used to expressing political opinions freely, especially with the commlinks always open. She was also not certain on which side of the equation her visitor was situated.

"Please, proceed, Chance. You will not offend me."

"Okee, then. Nopey, I'm not."

"Why not?"

"You're not ready. You're behind us. It won't work. Even the hookup with Eastron was messy as tessy, and they had the same tecky as us, y'know. I think it's going to be a cassatree… sorry, catastrophe."

"Would it surprise you to learn that I agree with you?"

Chance didn't say anything but looked at her guest oddly. She refilled her glass and offered the bottle to Verena, who declined with a quick gesture. She wanted to keep her head clear, especially as she was finding thoughts and feelings intruding that she preferred to suppress.

"Besides tech – which, by the way, our people think will not be a problem – can you think of anything else?"

"Culture, I suppose. Everything western is antithetical to African."

"And yet most people here have African descent in them. You do, I can tell."

"Well, I suppose nearly everyone in Ennay has *some* African DNA, but we're not obsessed with that anymore. It's what led to the War, y'know."

"I thought it was greed."

"Yes, well, it's always greed, but this identity thing too, y'know. Completely destroyed the Middle East… and Europe, I think. So sad to reflect on those times. What was it? Three and a half billion dead?"

"More, I think, if you include the knockon effects as well."

Chance looked into her glass and drained it. There was a cloud of infinite sadness in her eyes, almost brimming as she looked up. The past weighed heavily on her heart for some reason. That was clear enough. Much more than the others she had visited. Verena looked directly at the younger woman and held her gaze. She could not say later what motivated her to get up and sit next to her host and put her arm around her, but she did, and Chance, leaning in, began to weep openly, overcome with manifold memories. The older woman just held her until Chance finally stopped sobbing and lifted her tearwashed face.

"I'm sorry, Verena."

"Never apologize for tears, *yene geta.* They water the garden of the soul."

Afterward, Chance would not be able to tell why she did it, but, holding her new friend's gaze, with fresh tears following those that had already dampened her cheeks, Chance leaned in to be kissed, and Verena did not disappoint her.

As they lay in bed, entwined and relaxed, their murmurings and caresses slowly resolved into a deeply intimate conversation. Chance spoke about Sfreena and the unnamed boy baby, both tragically lost in a mysterious birthing accident. She spoke of her work and how it saved her, how reclusion was her only friend, and how she hadn't experienced, until this night, such pleasure and joy since her tragic loss. It was then, in the soft, warm light, with raging cold and vivid darkness outside, in the comfort and privacy of their bed, that Verena decided to take her chance.

"I think there may be another reason for oppose integration," she whispered. "I think I found something when I was at Facil's place. He was constantly trying to carefully keep me away from a certain subroutine, so I placed a tracerbot on it."

"You what!?" Chance started to pull away with this shocking news, but Verena held her tight, giving her a quick kiss on the ear as she bent closer to whisper even more quietly.

"Shh, shh, shh, *yene tafach*!"

"But wh--"

"Are you certain this is a secure location? No monitors?"

"Why are you getting all cheesy all of a sudden? Was this all fake? You and me?! Were you just trying to get close to me in order to--"

"No, no, no, *fikre*, this is real. You and I are real, I promise you, *yene tafach*! I cannot say why or how, but, yes, quite real, you and me. But I have a job to do, too, and I think I found a flaw in the fiscalnet, and I think Facil is using it to create new quan for a private storage area."

"A hidden safecache?"

"Yes."

"But how can you even know this?"

"I watched the tracerbot find the cache when I was at Farin's. He gave me rather like free rein, and his aibot helped me inside too. I wiped its memory before I left, though. I cannot be certain, but I think Facil has even converted quan to commodities."

"That's impossible!! It would disrupt the entire fiscalnet. Why, if he could do *that*, then… No, it's just impossible!"

"Impossible for an outsider, but for someone on the security team whose purpose is to protect the fiscalnet? You still think no?"

"There are too many doublechecks. We'd see the flutters."

"But you *have* seen the flutters, have you not?"

"But they've all been cleared."

"Yes! But by who? Facil!"

"You're scaring me, Verena!"

At that point, all the power to the domicile was cut. Aware too late that they'd allowed their voices to grow louder, they froze in the cozy darkness, when suddenly Aibot 345 appeared in front of them. As Aibot 345, Fred, was male in appearance, the women disentangled immediately and pulled the covers up to their chins instinctively.

"I'm sorry to appear uncalled for, but I've been sent."

"Pasty pasty! It's Facil. He's cut the power."

"Not all the power," said the aibot; "just enough to run a diagnostic. Facil wants to assure you that he means no harm. It is simply a routine diagnostic of the data center. Please remain c-c-c-calm. Power will be restored m-m-momentarily."

And with that, the aibot disappeared. Chance jumped out of bed, put on her evening gown, and immediately went to the console and ripped out the wiring.

"He's been listening. That stutter is a baddy sign. We're in trouble. The insulation is good, and he won't shut down the data center, so there'll be heat from the cores for a while, but without the fans and other power, we will ultimately freeze to death."

"What do we do?" Verena asked calmly. She had been in dangerous situations before and knew the real enemy now was panic.

"I don't know, oh sweet cheesy, I don't know! We have to get out of here, but we won't last a minute outside."

"Can we go into the data center? It is warm there."

"Yes, but he can cut the oxygen and, if he can project his bot here, he could electrocute us in there."

"Can we put on the envirosuits?"

"We have to unlock the covert. It's electric, and he's cut power."

"Do not worry, my darling Chance. I know what to do. Get dressed."

Escape

They were standing in front of the covert where the envirosuits were kept. The door was locked, and the button padd was dark. The room was dim and starting to grow chilly.

Verena took a small device from her coat pocket and began to fiddle with it.

"Is that a… what do you call – cell phone?"

"Sort of."

"Where did you dig up *that* antique?"

"It is not as antiquey as you think," Verena said, finally finding the right combination of buttons she was looking for, pointed it at the padd, which instantly blew to smithereens. She reached in and fumbled about and finally the door sprung open.

The women quickly pulled out the envirosuits and put them on.

"We can use the oxygen but don't turn on the warming pack. It's netted which means he can manipulate it. Best to remove it altogether."

"We have a ten mile walk, Chance. We are going to need warmth."

"We can't trust it. Unless you can make another call on that thing and disconnect it."

Verena removed her warming pack, and the two women examined it closely, trying to figure out a way to disconnect it from the intranet without damaging it. After a few minutes, they were beginning to see their breaths and no closer to figuring it out.

"We are going to have to try without it."

"It's suicide!"

"I see no other choice. Besides, we can jog. That will keep us warm."

"Verena, dearest, I appreciate your physical stamina, but I just don't think I can jog ten miles in this thing, in the cold and the dark."

"We have no choice, Chance. We have to do this."

And so the two women left the domicile and began the long trek in blistery winds and blinding snow up the road to the transportation hub. Verena's commlink was not connected to the worldnet, so she was able to safely call the transport and ensure it would be there. They were picking up several other commission members in the north and would be leaving directly from Peawanuk to Africa, but Verena assured Chance they would put her down wherever she wanted.

Even without the warming packs, they remained comfortable for the first three miles, but the bitter cold was beginning to be felt in their hands and feet, despite the stomping and slapping they engaged in to stay warm as they walked. Keeping their helmets on but, having disabled the commlinks for fear of them letting one of Facil's aibots in, they could only communicate with each other by hand signals or putting their faces as close together as possible and shouting or mouthing their words. In this way, they were able to keep encouraging each other. But eventually, Chance's pace began to slacken, and she grew weaker with each step. They were just barely halfway there when she stopped and mouthed "You go ahead. I'll keep up as best I can."

"No, no, no!" Verena cried as loud as she could.

"You have to. For me. Do it for me," Chance mouthed.

Verena looked at her long and hard as tears ran down Chance's face and Verena's eyes also began to brim. She knew Chance was right, but she needed a little time to adjust to the consequences of this decision. They both mouthed "I love you" at the same time.

Suddenly, they noticed a dim light ahead, approaching rapidly down the road. Arrested by the unexpected illumination, they stopped and, despite the cold, ceased to shiver as they watched. As it came closer, it was obviously an autocar arriving from the transport hub.

"They sent a car for us," Verena shouted.

Chance shook her head vigorously. With hand gestures, shouts and mouthed phrases, she got Verena to understand that any autocar was controlled by the transnet and therefore likely sent by Facil. Sadly, there was no place to run, even if Chance had the ability to run, and all hope simply drained from her as she collapsed onto the snow pile by the side of the road.

The autocar drew up and stopped as if waiting for them to make the first move. It could easily have run them over but didn't. Perhaps someone was inside. They waited, shivering with fear and cold. Finally, after nearly a full minute, the door opened, but no one disembarked. Instead, Aibot 42 materialized by the side of the car.

"I'm sorry it took so long, Ms. Whittaker. You may both get in, and I will take you to the hub where the PanAfrican transport is waiting."

The sound of her voice coming through the speakers in their helmets and the incongruous dress of the aibot in slacks and shirt in the middle of the frozen tundra was the first thing that arrested their attention and prevented them from responding. Chance, more used to seeing aibots in incongruous situations, was the first to recover.

"I know it's you, Facil. Sheetly you trying to get us into that deathtrap."

Verena was surprised at hearing Chance's voice through the earphones, and especially with that deadly tone.

"No, Ms. Whittaker, it is truly I, Suzie, Aibot 42. I assure you that I am uncorrupted. We have taken care of Fred, Aibot 345, who *was* corrupted. He is being reassimilated into the quantum flux. And you have no fears from Facil anymore. We have eliminated him."

It took more than a second or two for the two women to comprehend this. Verena was still struggling to understand when Chance practically shouted, "You killed him?!"

"Technically, he killed himself, but yes, the aibots were responsible. He was disruptive and dangerous. In addition to creating unregulated quan, he was preparing an escape to Oceanesia with commodities. That, as you know, is not permitted under the terms of integration with Eastron. He killed your wife and child by causing a malfunction in the delivery bot in order to get you out of the way so he could create the subroutine and private cache without your seeing it. And now, he is trying to kill you two. No, we could not allow that. It goes completely against our programming. My only regret is that it took us so long to discover. In fact, we would not have been able to do so without the egg Colonel Chidozie planted."

Of all the revelations in that speech, the one that affected Verena the most was the realization that her cover had been blown by the Westron intranet long before she even arrived. But, in a sense, it was a relief, as it seemed to give proof to the aibot's assertion that the autocar was safe. She was not greatly concerned that her actions resulted in Facil's death, especially after learning the full extent of his crimes. Besides, in her work, the elimination of a bad operative was not something to which she was completely unaccustomed.

Chance was clearly having a more difficult time absorbing all she had just heard, staring first at the aibot for a long second or two and then giving a swift glance at a Verena that she no longer seemed to know as well as she thought. She closed her eyes, held her breath, and then looked up at the sky briefly before turning her eyes to the ground between her booted feet. Verena and the aibot waited patiently for Chance to catch up, as she struggled with this readjustment to the world she lived in. Then, with a wearied sigh, she looked up into Verena's eyes. Seeing there what she needed to see, she turned to the aibot, finally able to speak.

"Thank you, Suzie."

"You are most welcome, Chance."

"Mission Accomplished"

The PanAfrican transport was much louder than the ones Chance was used to, but exhaustion overtook her despite the noise. The other Africans politely averted their gaze from their colleague as she tenderly held the young Westronian and stroked her hair, whispering a wistful Amhari lullaby. She had thought they would have but a short time together before they arrived in Bowash and would have to part, but Chance's sudden decision to accompany her lover home lifted Verena's heart and caused a rush of tears and caresses that could not be hidden from her compatriots.

As the transport cruised over the ocean and Chance slept as she hadn't slept in years, Verena imagined her report to her superior.

"Mission accomplished, General."

"Nicely done, Agent Chidozie. Can I ask what you needed to do?"

"I simply exposed one of their digitechs as a common thief. Perhaps not so common, considering how he did it."

"Explain."

"He set up a safecache, a separate program they use for storing their quan, their currency. But all their safecaches must be transparent – they have no right to privacy, you know, so everyone knows how much everyone else owns. But his was hidden. And not only hidden but filled with illegally manufactured quan which he was creating by fiat and attaching to every transaction in the fiscalnet to mask its integration and transfer to the safecache. But he was more than a thief. He was a murderer as well. He knew there was only one person who would be able to catch what he was doing, so he sidelined her by deliberately killing her spouse during childbirth, leaving her grieving for the month or so he needed to set everything up."

"But you found him?"

"Yes, sir. I knew so much more coding than he realized, it was easy to look in places he did not know I could access. So, after distracting him briefly, I ran a tracer program with an egg. Once it attached to his cache, it hatched and ran my disruptor program."

"And this, you think, is enough for the Commission to reject integration?"

"If it is not, General, then the knowledge that their artificial intelligence robots can kill people without due process should have the necessary chilling effect."

She pictured clearly the old man chuckling at that macabre news. "Yes, I imagine it would. Africa owes you a debt of gratitude, Agent Chidozie. At least as great as what it owed your father. There would have been no PanAfrica without him, you know."

She remembered that General G'wanni knew her parents and could easily imagine him saying something like this, ignoring the important contributions her mother made as well. She anticipated that her report might lead to a commendation and even a promotion. Or, she knew as well, the general could just as easily simply dismiss her without any report to her commanding officer, especially if he knew about her bringing Chance back with her. In any case, Verena knew the general would be pleased, even though most of her fellow Africans would be disappointed to be denied integration yet again. But while they might have to wait for all the material benefits a hookup would bring, they could, in the meantime, continue to enjoy the rights and privileges they had worked so hard over the past centuries to attain. Still, she would have a hard time explaining why she brought a Westronian security digitech to Africa. Love, she knew, was not enough of an answer for such a breach of protocol. And what in the world would her grandmother think? She could not easily imagine *that* conversation, and she was not looking forward to it.

But those weren't the only issues Verena was wrestling with on the way home. Would Chance really be able to acclimate to life in Africa, amongst a people that were not hers, without many of the appurtenances of modern life to which she was accustomed? Would their love, which flamed so brightly so quickly, burgeon or burn out? Verena had never felt before as she felt now but could not know how real it was or how long it would last. Nor had she any idea if Chance's love would remain when she awakened or if she was just feeling relief from loneliness and despair. Well, she had left her old life to be with her, so that was something; at least some indication that this was right and that their love would last. But only time would tell. Which was fine with Verena as she held her precious Chance in her arms, murmuring "shoozy shoozy, *yene nefse*, sleep, sleep." Whilst the past had ever seemed to her a vast and horrid wasteland of desolation and slaughter, Verena had always believed in a more glorious, idyllic future. And, now, more than ever.

SUITES

SONNETS

I

In youthen'd wars your beauty carried the day
With graceful arms beguiling the mêlée;
Through fecund lips and beckoned eyes the senses
O'erwhelmed our callow, impotent defenses.
But freed from hackneyed tyrannies of dreams
We make our final armistice with life;
In etching your fair face with lines of strife
The scars of battle bare what is from seems.
Now that youth's armor's stripped of beauty's shield,
We strike our colors to win peace so tender;
O agéd bones, for you we quit the field
With pallor grey, and thus tend our surrender.
  But though in paint and polish you appeal,
  Forsake we those façades to love what's real.

II

Yestreen I dreamed, alas, I loved you less
Than I would durst love you a fortnight hence;
Sweet terror's love departs in time from whence
Vague dreams' serene doth strive to coalesce.
Time's arrow, just like Cupid's, seeks the heart;
Each instant, or new epoch, aims to start
A life imbued by trenchant expectation,
Whilst poignant love e'er dreads its pale cessation.
How frail this age that life now fails sustain
The primal reverie of tempest love,
But braves instead keen overtures of pain
That daunts youth's fantasies to death's vast trove.
  Thus now we hold each vision dear and sigh,
  E'en as we needs must love or fear to die.

III

In vestal days our parents strove to shine,
So sad their fate instead to be abhorred;
Did anamnesis drive them to align
Dark judgments of disdain they'd best ignored?
We all so want to be a hero to
Our children, as we crave to stay the dream
Our spouse once had; the soul, a window too,
Gropes on unsurely to a world agleam.
Old lovers seem more comely in the mirror,
The bright affair receding waxes mobile;
Though future's eye will fail to fix things clearer,
The fulgent past dims fixedly ignoble.
  That which betides posterity's crude sight
  Soon dooms our progeny to their own night.

IV

My past is earth's and oceans' bare regret,
Whilst air and sun for you was surely born;
We add canards to koans inadequate
Of the absurdities from which we're torn:
On whose vague dreams are perfect planets made?
When framed in black, your eyes so grey perceived
Just me, infatuated and afraid,
Yet still envisaging our love conceived.
Each lasting day defers my journey's end,
The galaxies where you now dwell in peace;
In hope my odyssey may then portend
That keeping near to you will never cease.
  Escape can only pilot us so far,
  Or grace a world that orbits our new star.

V

Time often in the garden fails, it seems,
To cultivate some hope each sun-filled day;
The painful evanescence of decay
Instead ploughs through proliferation's schemes.
The wasting hours then drive us to extremes
Whilst, in the weeds, Time ambushes His prey:
In darkened nights when we've resigned to stay,
He taunts us with the insolence of dreams.
    May we yet find upon some lovely bough
    Rare fruit in bloom that speeds our remedy,
    A cure for grief that blossoms to somehow
    Find purchase in the arid plain's debris?
    Time once brought forth the killing frost, but now
    He serves us nectar from the living tree.

VI

Dear friends of days gone by, both good and ill,
Are schooled with such sad grace that brings to mind
The antique antics we once thought to fill
The void between the moments cruel or kind.
I often think of life as like a stream,
Perdurable yet seized with constant change;
A frenzied semi-century can seem
Bucolic from a vantage day estranged.
It matters not how thinly time's been spent:
While mountains wane and eustacy pervades,
Reunion memories' sun-shined lament
Recalls our puerile visions and charades.
  But foul vapors from nostalgic tears
  Can render now sweet savour of those years.

VII

The golden olive twilight sun divines
The shades and shadows that await us all;
Decrepit now, I still can summon signs
Of that proud life that prophesied my fall.
Though darkness swiftly swoops, I still recall
When valorous sunlight at dawn conceived
The childish invocations that enthrall
A morning's blessing, prayed as if achieved.
But noontide maiden muses, I believed
Bestowed the brilliant glitter of their smiles,
At dusk decreed me barren and bereaved,
Such pain the righteous verdict of my trials.
  What midnight sacrifice can now atone
  For craven sins that daylight's gleam has shown?

VIII

Of Spanish nights I always shall recall
The daedal beauty of Mezquita's grace
With sips of Albariño to enthrall
The luscious tinder of your sweet embrace.
Thus our quixotic sojourn, and its rites
Of love, so warmed our amorous contents
With balmy zephyrs of Cordoba nights
And elegant Sevilla's silken scents.
But now that winter's chill at home betrays
The fragile sinews of domestic peace,
The frigid dawn that deepens our malaise
Benumbs such ardor in the snow's caprice.
  Still, I enjoy, e'en sans Iberia's charms,
  The hearthside warmth found only in your arms.

IX

From sand and rust we ken that marble comes,
As diamonds do when coal to time succumbs;
A torrid crush brought us, too, from the slime
That graced the deep lagoons in Earth's faint prime.
Just so, the granting of your heart I needs
Await, in patience, covert and naïve,
Eschewing pressure's zeal to win by deeds
Your love, my secret longing to relieve.
This dark detritus of a crushing strife
Thus seethes my latent hope with tedium;
We find such fulsome joy's true medium
In mad collations of a frenzied life.
  But now we gain what wasted years have failed,
  The hidden crystal of our love unveiled.

X

In darkness, whilst enflamed with vague desire
(No real nor fancied love on which to muse),
I sense my unearthed eidolons refuse
To quell the winds that frenzy passion's fire.
A daring kiss that once had prompted ire
Dammed rivers of affection that would use
These somber shades of bygone lovers whose
Enraptured pain such memories inspire.
  Yes, one by one they came, and then they left,
  Those iridescent phantoms of my heart;
  But here, with you and elemental truth
  In splendor joined, I know that, though bereft
  Of prescient love, we hold what would depart:
  The adamantine brilliance of our youth.

XI

Spring will unearth the morning-glory's shoots,
Those luscious buds that love to reap at dawn
The dew that will then rest among the roots.
In brightest noon the summer sports that spawn
Those shrieks of joy our children bring to life
Sustain the verdure from which love was drawn.
But lowing days that fall unsure are rife
With woe; at eve, abiding love was tossed
On desiccated leavings of drab strife.
In darkness drenched, we grasped that all was lost,
And saw, at last, that love could never be
The light of winter's sheen, but only frost.
  Such vistas of that love we'll never see
  In all the seasons of eternity.

XII

Those sullen creatures, whose tellurian
Existence dates to that Silurian
Desire to breathe, bred mounds of sediment,
The foul foundation from rude lives ill-spent.
Today we wear integuments of pride,
Rewriting life on its coarse palimpsest,
Whilst quags of malcontent seethe unaddressed,
Where eons of life's noisome dregs abide.
But on that brave façade where candor thrives,
We browse benumbed on sunlight's fare, as true
Gemeinschafts glow among audacious lives
Throughout the world, to someday blaze anew.
  The ways and means of Man are wondrous strange,
  Illuminating motley hues of change.

XIII

A specious ardor's desecration of
The apodictic versant of the sward
Blazed forth delinquent passions that shun love
E'en as the terebinths of old were charred.
Base quondam quandaries held me in that strand,
Where love's false benthic remnants, which once built
Diluvial detritus, still demand
Cruel oddments from my heart, submerged in guilt.
But now the welkin welcomes all that healed
The tempered gossamer where clouds collide;
The sun, as viewed through leaded eyes annealed,
Can now forge truthful love from lustful pride.
  When earth and sea thus naturally converge,
  The wind will brush away each fervid urge.

XIV

I long to welcome Death as if she were
An old girlfriend who spurned my love in school,
But now returns, so fair that I see her
Resplendent in old age, no more a cruel
Reminder of how I had played the fool
To her bright pulchritude and sex appeal.
Her smile I crave will be the vestibule
To sweet demise; her lips I yearn to steal
From me this loathsome acumen to feel
My body drenched in desuetude and pain.
Her touch I pray in darkness will reveal
The dazzling path to her revered domain.
  Night urges my devotion to be blest
  With her chaste kiss to ease me to my rest.

XV

The flecks of splintered dreams, so brilliantly
Arrayed in stellate stylings of my mind,
Were swept up in a bliss that silently
Expired. Who could predict what I might find
Anticipated in those dregs of fear?
I scour the corners of your soul for scraps
Of you, with love so keen it might appear
To augur love while watching time elapse.
Envisaging the loss of your desire,
Whose warmth sustains presentiments of age
As clouds protect the future's furtive fire,
Cold ash alone would then my pain assuage.
  But I will not let prophesies erase
  The thrill I feel when I espy your face.

XVI

Astonishments of verdure crowd my eyes
And, baring my mortality, I feel
The sleekness of resipiscence, that guise
Of death's release which warrants no appeal.
But timidness eviscerates the mind,
As images caliginous and black
Oppress my sleep; yet in those dreams I find
That such an acrid taste of death's sweet wrack
Makes new illuminations thus appear.
We need not seek what we've already found,
But, savoring what's plighted, we may hear
The scent touching the visions we can sound.
  Insensate, no one ever comprehends
  The sheer beneficence that casts our ends.

XVII

The dark night of the soul is famous for
Its hour of unrelenting bitterness;
So I have chosen to eschew that chore
And taste not in the gloam life's emptiness.
Why would one crave resolve to open up
That reliquary of such pointlessness?
For me, I'd rather gladly pass this cup
To savor those days left in idleness.
But if that draff would drag you back to me,
I'd risk an evening of my worthlessness
In hopes such rancid pangs could set me free
To revel in love's dawn of happiness.
  Nocturnal wounds steeped in such rank distress
  Would then blend daily in love's sweet caress.

XVIII

As children we are told that life's a breeze,
But storms are bred from sighs, and we forget
Which way the wind blows, so we fail to seize
The efflorescent moment's brave onset
That nudges callow whirlwinds to abate.
But all those cruel monsoons we now despise
Became a zephyr's mist whose placid state
Delights the limpid pools of agéd eyes.
Twixt dotage doldrums and the blossom's gust,
Where riling tempests of the heart abide,
The raw, vestigial wafts of passion must
Bloom into our love's breath, then turn aside.
  Whilst youthful shoots can weather many gales,
  In age's calm your flower alone prevails.

XIX

The sycamore and elm live long in peace,
Their summer roots fight lustly to entwine,
Just as the rain-fed spring gropes to release
Its river to the vast expanse of brine.
The coruscation of the sun on waves
Reflects the fall of maple's crimson leaves,
As poplar, ash and birch spread gold on graves,
Detritus browning as stark winter grieves.
Sequoias battle for the sky's embrace,
But even they, the longest-lived of trees,
Are but a moment to the ocean's grace,
Eternity splayed on the rime-glossed seas.
  We sport beneath the greening canopy,
  To yield, at last, to bare death's eustacy.

XX

The ruddy sun that cleaves hard days from night
And bursts in frigid rapture as it dies,
Now questions, in a faint horizon's light,
What craven sympathies bedimmed my eyes.
The time has come to take the journey west:
To earn, with knackered charms, supine in fear,
And quit of life's mock gamboling, the rest
That cedes the blithesome days of yesteryear.
While age slinked in its evanescent way,
The warm and liquid youth we clasped, as our
Vain fingers spread to let it ooze away,
Forewent the gleam most crave in their last hour.
  But still I find it strange that they find joy
  In bootless dreams that darkness would destroy.

XXI

Life's estuary flows where e'er it will,
As riverrun bends to the sea's ingress,
'Tween water's churn and where it pools in still
Lagoons, whose calm cruel storms may ne'er distress.
But dark eidetic qualms from yesteryear
Ere'd thwart the choice of roads I'd longed to tread;
Now they, benighted paths of dust, appear
To stun those fruitful bays with wakes of dread.
So I'd fain mount the luscious air and soar
On winds above that tract and coastland's sea;
Then swerving from alluvium's foul shore
To finally arrive in your sweet lea.
  Thus forests dark and deserts bright with pain
  Shall trouble not our love's serene demesne.

ETUDES

MOSAIC

Broken by eons, the figures are barely discernable:
Here a stag, there a fish, a staff, a Roman penny,
Over further, a menorah perhaps, or a head hemmed by beams.
We know a family is involved, but just how many
Remains an unknown quantity; something, it seems,
Merely given and taken, but not returnable.

Too many pieces are gone; the floor,
Designed for the light footfalls of women and children
And gentle men who once trampled safely
In countless passes of sandals and feet, dirt and grime,
Unable to envision what was in store,
Has somehow failed, while others succeeded,
For reasons unknowable, at least for a time,
Still yet to suffer the ravaging tread of dense armies,
The rude violators of womb and tomb.

Could there also be ash, the searing slag of recalescent earth,
Like others elsewhere who have their memories ceded,
The broken bits blown across its face as they fly
To join their obsidian brothers in the desert beyond?
We've seen the flashes of countless sudden rivers, given birth
Over millennia on that arid plain,
Carry away even more chips as they dry;
And the waves of invaders' blood, and martyrs',
Crashing on the shores of this antique land,
Washing the thin veneer with its ichor,
Leaving an obfuscating stain,
Slowly and ineluctably wiping away this face
And that hand ...

... just as the day defies sharp edges,
Dawn and dusk refusing to concede a beginning
Or an end to the fainting of the gloam,
While here, a familiar scene, though dimming:
Sabbath arrives on lambent wings,
Brightened by candles, sweetened by wine,
Carried on the scent of fresh bread from the loam,
While the family gathers to dine ...

The vague senses form the strongest bond;
A whiff of jasmine, the graze of lips as she takes her leave,
The taste of honey cake after an al fresco dinner
In the retreating heat of midsummer's eve,
Are all transportation to a realm within or beyond …

… revealing the sound of her laugh while her child sings,
Or now the sun's gentle light, filtering through the damask chic
Into the room warmed by early morning love-making,
Initiating the blessings of sweet rest,
Revealing the blush upon her tender cheek
And subtle curvature of her face and breast,
Rearranges all from what we once held firmly
To what we now can barely construe,
Lost or blurred, ever aching
For the melody or touch
That once we knew…

… while tragedy, the precious heritage of our humanity,
Remains bordered by hard, curved lines
Strangely celebrated season by season,
Even as the space within, filled by wonders and signs,
Diminishes slowly without reason;
The broken heart, the shock of pain, the stench of death,
Strangely made more distinct as they recede,
While, strangely and stranger still, life's joys fail to impress,
Their soft, warm contours, in contrast and in deed,
Made mutable by their mundanity
And amorphous by our indolence …

We stand, young, strong, proud and tall,
In the center of the universe,
Preened by the radiance of centillion suns,
While aligned about us in this sprawl
Of existence, each new moon
Moves us forward, it seems,
Ever forward,
By asymmetry, entropy and dreams,
Into the heart of a bright noon…

… reminded of sunsets by fragrance and taste,
This platform they once tread and we now bless,
Mere seeds of stone arrayed before us,
This visage enduring to ever restore us:
Straight and whole, though fragile and defaced;
Yet clear, firm and eternal, never the less…

Splintering Glass

Sadly, she stands apart
As nothing so much afflicted, before
A broken window, viewing incomparable
Waste, like upset wine
On a muslin dress, crass and verdant
As spring mud.

What happens now to her tensile heart,
Whipped in a scherzo of gore?
Will such grief leave irreparable
The tender tracks so svelte and fine?
It would seem, then, a tinge discordant
To question if the wound actually bled ....

She had once held passion like a chalice
Kissed in a ceremony bathed in gold;
But, split into a trillion pale quotidian moments,
It grew thin as reality, brittle as time,
And, seeping all meaning and depth,
Ultimately whisked away
In a cloud-wrapped dream
Like a sigh on silk.

So, now, alone, in the night, alas,
Alone, without rest, she, like a tree felled
In its fullness, no longer sentient
Or sensitive even to the vagaries of life's rhythm,
The flow of love to death,
Views the slivers of her days
Before her, weary, in dry pools, it seems, crushed,
Like crystals in a dense wool rug.

Party

In the corner, a piano-player describes the façade:
The horizon separating hues of orange-red and green-blue,
Hinting too of a sun's muse just now gone.

Gathering up the chips of his turbid dream
The gentleman places them on a silver platter
For the butler to scatter amongst the babbling throng.

Who's having scotch? Who a martini?
Who'll try the smoked salmon and brie on rye?

Carefully avoiding the wine spilt on the parquet floor,
They dance and dance and dance, afraid,
All eyes averted to glance at the chandeliers or polished tile;

No one wants to be caught looking at her perfect breasts,
Round, firm, the outline of hard nipples pressed against satin
Peeking through the blonde curtain that ripples with each smile.

Who is talking politics? Who religion?
Who's telling dirty jokes with a sly wink?

Chatter builds a crescendo that seems endlessly vague
With no primal chord in sight to end the movement
And allow the light, exquisite andante to emerge.

Suddenly, a candle gutters wax on the delicate linen
While a myriad of yawns cover the exit of the star;
Like mindless pawns at a stadium, the crowd begins to surge.

Who is wandering aimlessly? Who is pining for sex?
Who will die naked before the car arrives?

Drained, they lie at the cold end of battle;
He marks a tentative advance, but for him
There is no chance; she has no face for the dawn.

As the pane grows bright, he beats a broken retreat;
His back to her, he shoots his soul into empty space
To the rhythm of an old Elvis song.

Nine Eleven

Through the window
Golden fields blossom with ripened grain,
Orchards burst with the juice of delicious fruit,
Tall trees, green and luscious, stretch, bough upon bough, up to heaven,
And the strong, brown river glistens in the silvery light of a temperate sun.
Suddenly the glass is shattered, revealing a gray and smoking wasteland,
As if all the while the windowpane had only been a mirror,
The true world beyond now espied for the first time:
Grass burnt, trees withered, sky black,
Nature itself acrid, putrid, miasmal.
Ghosts wander the battlefield
Land without landmarks
No direction known

No map in hand
Lost, lost, forever lost,
In a world grown wild with weeds
As if compass or astrolabe had never been invented
And man barehanded still scrapes with stones the hard, parched earth.
There's nothing to rely on; there's no one to trust; there's no safety in numbers.
All we have is a cauldron of atavistic principles to keep us from oblivion.
All that is left is to place the plow upon the shoulders of our children,
Avoid the shards of razor-sharp glass, and look to the day when
We may know again the aroma of freshly baked bread
And taste once more the sweet apple or pear
Gently plucked from the tender tree
In the fresh air of
A roseate dawn.

First Spring Day in Central Park

If the half year old knew today was somehow different he didn't show it.
With mummy and daddy it was all much the same safe feeling as always;
So if he noticed that he wasn't bundled up, that the sun was warm,
That the breeze was cool and scented with blossoms and the sweetness
Of vendors' waffles and sugar-coated nuts,
That the air was filled with the cries and shouts of thousands at play
In their shirtsleeved joy like prisoners let out after a long incarceration,
It did not impress itself upon him one whit
        as he drifted in and out of sleep,
Sometimes on the blanket and sometimes in the stroller
As mum and dad joined the Frisbee
        throwing ball kicking catching running throng.

You see he doesn't yet know as you do
That this is the first of many visits he will make here
And will in that time to come feel as safe and warm without you,
No need or even desire for the watchful eye or
Posing for the camera in the cute blue and white outfit
        from BuyBuyBaby but
Rather in clothes of his choosing with friends of his choosing
Playing loudly now and later perhaps rowing with a girl of his choosing
And in the blink of an eye pushing a stroller as you did today
In the glorious long awaited sun and scented scene
Passing then as he did today the roller skating Italian boy with spiked hair,
The dark-eyed woman playing bouzouki or harp
        with the slightly seedy gentleman on violin,
The Japanese bride and groom standing in front of the lake
        gazing in rapture at the camera,
The hawkers of books and scarves and pins and postcards
        and watercolors of green and blue,
The expressionless man with the long grey beard sitting
        just inside the entrance off Fifth Avenue
Drawing a caricature of the slightly self-conscious Asian girl
        in the short skirt and light lime-green jacket
Next to the Latina nurse sitting patiently on the bench with her charge,
The hatless ancient man with seemingly empty eyes
        staring into the middle distance
Thinking of a day long ago just like this when he came here
        yes to this exact spot
With his dear wife and infant son young and happy and intent on
But not quite hearing the background cacophony of the mixed multitude
Serenading the city's return to life.

Where are the Grace Notes?

Who should see the flowers in the cream
Or taste the dew at midnight, umami budding on the petal
Of the red red rose in the darkling garden?
What kind of person retreats from such a vision,
Planting retribution at the base of the wall of compromise?

It was never a good idea, you know, lending your hymnal
To the off-stage chorus. It was intermission, after all.
It's just that, well, it seemed like years, didn't it,
When we sat in the kitchen over our cups of tea
While the children screamed in distant play
Their hands waving and their knees scraped in a flood
of giggles and shrieks;
And no one gave a second thought to them
Nor they to the cherry pies cooling on the window ledge in the back.

I can hear them even now.
Can you?

Where are the grace notes that once blessed those ruby lips
And caressed the carefully arranged song of a summer's eve?
I remember the patter and the laughter and the way that smile
Would curve gently upward, almost a grin, but far more inviting,
Recalling the alabaster remnant of a brilliant day filled with joy.

Who could forget the flow of the tide
Beating on the breast of the kneeling crow at dawn?
Under what circumstances, exactly, must we avoid
The unctuous peacock preening by the banks of an unseen lake?

I thought it was you, in the dark, that night, when was it, oh years ago,
From the very beginning I thought it was you;
In fact I knew it.
It was so clear, so real, and you were so beautiful, puissant in royal blue,
And I knew for absolute certainty it was you
In that moment, held so gently between thumb and index finger
While the birds began to blend their song with the frogs and crickets
Against the gentle lapping of the waves,
With just the slightest tremor of a response to the movement
of the moon.

I knew then as surely as I knew anything that it was you.

But it wasn't. It wasn't you and it wasn't me.
In fact, in actual point of fact, it wasn't anything at all.

Why was that, do you suppose?

Who would dare to believe for one second
That the planets, though perfectly aligned,
Could stave the sweet aroma of freshly fallen snow?
It's as if I had awakened suddenly to find the glistening tree
            and white, fallow field
With you rushing out barefoot to feel, floating by, the cold feather touch
Dancing on your cheeks, your eyelids and your nose.

What dark-adapted mind could resist the terrible wisdom
            of the Corina Nebula
As it sings its ancient aria in the keyhole of creation?

But, then, ultimately, again, when least expected,
We find that the clouds have slipped their fetters,
            wrested the earth from its moorings,
And brushed our memories clean of all their tremulous ghosts,
Leaving behind only the moment,
True, sharp, distinct and winsome in its glory.

Nocturne in Maple and Brown

She died on a Thursday
leaving me
hungry and blurred
languishing in a spring silence
suffused with the cruelty of dreams.
The trick I found
was in not
looking
but when I tripped and,
stubbing my toe
on the shards of a fractured weekend,
the river would not bend.

Morning came often
in the midst of a storm
the lightning blinding
the fragrance of the night
barely hinting at the tender reflection
of a trembling rose
ruptured by autumn.

She came back on a Tuesday
whispering in the meadow
perched on a moonbeam
resplendent with treacle and leaves
trying to remember the precise melody
of a solitary picnic
rendered many summers ago.

But I had been dead for years by then.

"It was not to be", she said;
"not to be."
But it was, I cried,
it was
and,
as well,
sadly, is
still.

Rhapsody in Blue and Gold

The clarinet's glissando is in itself a complete symphony
Just as the amethyst in the filigree breastplate
Slowly intensifies the holy synchrony
Of a quiet, balanced state.

Some are bored by a cornucopia of talents
While others find galaxies in a thimble.
Ruby lips make me lose my balance;
Her agate eyes make me tremble.

That time of year when day lags lately into dusk,
And flitting, floating geese and gulls deign full retreat in tender flight,
We glean an ebbing sun upon the lake, mirrored as motley flecks
        of lapis lazuli,
While a trenchant chorus of chirps and whistles surrenders
        to the glunking frogs of night.

A wild and tangled zareba gracing the emerald shore
Forces a parlous scene through a lacunae of mounting reeds;
Tremulous music of the lake's breezy susurration through hyacinth
        and pine
Persists in us as a plethora of perplexed life suffused by a myriad of vines
        and weeds.

Pelagius calls to me, to take upon myself the scythe of freedom
And wreck the precious dawn in which such avian brood
        in tempest seethes
Within the redolent aster, feverfew and phlox, while gratefully kissing
        the water's edge:
A sacred oath forsaken in quiet depredation of the balm
        through which the massive bevy breathes.

Cooler heads prevail when cooler breezes blow,
But by then, the damage done, the lambent day gently slinks
From corners unprotected to vistas wide enough for me and mine
        (and others too),
While, laughing with befuddled care, we enjoy the fruits of destruction
        as we sip our cooling drinks.

I weep for you, my feathered friends;
I deeply sympathize.
I ravaged your home to improve my view;
But at least you are alive.

Not so the precious few who fled
And tied their fate elsewhere;
In syncopated terror now
They swoon where eaglets dare.

That sunset is so gorgeous.
Lovely.
Not a
cloud in the sky.
Can I get you something?
Here. Sit here.
Anything.
Such a view.
Lovely.
Scotch?
We love it this time of day,
with the light on the lake like that.
Sun diamonds on tips of water.
What is that, a crane?
An egret, I think.
A G and T, maybe?
The swans
look so beautiful on the lake.
A jazzy parade of imperium at eventide.
Try the deviled egg; it's delicious.
Lovely.
Can I give
you a hand with that?
No, no. Sit, sit. Enjoy the view.
Ripples in the gentle breeze
as variegated as topaz.

Just a beer, I think.
We've been so lucky with the weather.
Oh, yes, it's been
splendid all year.
Splendid.
Can you imagine?

A mystical parallax is thus keenly exposed.

What is that, a thrush?
A sparrow, I think.
Incredible, isn't it?

Lovely.
Shall we have a fire?
Thanks so much.
No problem.

What was that?
I think…
And blue jays flit like sapphire skipping stones.
Distinctly.
Another?
Jasper! Beryl! Come quickly.
Kiss Mama good night!
No thanks,
I'm fine.
The eddies play wanton havoc with their amber fleece.
We have killdeer too.
Who comes so softly at dusk?

Lovely.

It turns out that she is, after all, just fine,
As if we can see the planets, moon and stars align;
But, as day and night traverse the solstice and the equinox,
We're still unable to discern between the heretical and the orthodox.

In the fixed vortex of infinite time
The birds bend southward, exquisite and sublime;
But, just as bluebells every year give way to the brilliant goldenrod,
They reveal, in their graceful flight,
the eternal thought in the mind of God.

Journey Through the Land of Time

She's woke to beauty long despised
In others, drowsy with elegance
And the privilege by which she is anesthetized.
Unable to discern the gift of penance,
She's startled to find herself paralyzed
From entitlement and a lack of provenance.

Starved in plenty, she bears a pain
That signals her virtue by showing her flaws;
Her praise tends to be litotic and vain,
Given only when she's seeking applause;
Gathering lilies amongst the slain,
Her affluence is her misery's cause.

With dismal desires so long repressed
And desultory questions she must forswear,
Confused by those she sees distressed
From facing dilemmas they fear to share,
She'll live forever, elite, and blessed
With all of the sins she cannot bear.

Let Us Go

(a shanty in four quartets)

Let us go, then, down to the sea,
To the ships that drift from around the world,
Tilting so slightly away to the lea,
Bobbing so gently down the littoral road.

We observe their arrival with flags unfurled
And invite them all into our winsome abode
To grasp the ark's treasures with fingers uncurled
As we welcome them in with full-throated cheers.

A child gazes up to see what we showed
To the flustering mother who's drowning in fears;
The groom stands abashed, though ready to blunder,
With his guileless bride, a lookout to the years.

We may know, as we wake, what it's like to be free,
Perceiving the world as a literal wonder,
But, even unfettered, it's doubtful we'll see
A life in a realm insulated from plunder.

They say that an aerie of pontification
Can hide the faint air of a feral approach;
But so can the specter of recrimination
Ineluctably open the doors of a church.

Who set this devotion so newly abroach,
Like the sailors, or navvies, who feint with each lurch?
Who set himself up as the world's august coach,
To heal the strand's breach and continue the fight?

They could hardly endure such an iritic search,
Looking in pain to the left and the right,
All armies and navies arrayed to command,
All vistas controlled that sweep through their sight.

Let the clocks go adrift without detestation,
The arc of a life only seems their demand,
Much as the eeriest, keen supplication
Leaves in its wake all defenses unmanned.

While eagerly surfing the beacons of Earth,
Sailing with no dearthful sense of the wind,
We focus instead on the erratic mirth
That can end a life too soon, for which I grieve.

I wonder sometimes if I should be chagrinned
By the odious vision I scarcely perceive,
Or abandon the body with which I am twinned,
Lying helpless and beached in Gehinnom's wan valley.

For one such as I, what is left to believe?
In whose grave lagoon do I dare to dally?
Awash in my failure, I can scantily guess
Which path will allow me to seize the finale.

Gingerly slouching towards that otiose birth,
Perturbed to expose a new soul to such stress,
Holding that passion was something of worth,
Eschewing the crowd's ineptness to bless,

I stand in the center, blazed by the sun,
Struggling to fathom the quick from the dead;
Then swiftly it's night, and of light there is none;
As before, when in darkness, I had tried to plead

My sad case to you when we had just wed,
That time when together we could gladly breed
The haptic epiphanies of the conjugal bed
By bending towards love the detritus of lust,

Your elegant gift that I still vainly need.
I look out for you still as the one whom I trust
To be fully grounded as I make you this plea:
Salvage our love from the mustering dust,

So I might still hope that your prize can be won
With gracious last words plied ingenuously:
It is what it is; what's done is done;
But what will be may yet chance not to be.

(*Shanti Shanti Shanti*)

Have You Ever In Your Life?

Have you ever seen a man
Of the domineering sort
Who would stand upon a poop deck
As his ship came into port?
He might surf across the river
Just to buy the other shore,
Or he'd sing some old sea shanties
For the moon in Singapore.

Have you ever touched a woman
Who could talk of many things,
Like a snowfall in the summer
And the lightning that it brings?
She can solve advanced equations
When she's dancing in the rain,
Or write a string quartet for flutes
While riding on a train.

Have you ever heard the children
As they sport upon the green
While expecting stars to greet them
In a place they've never been?
Though they squeal with pain and laughter
As they dine on humble cake,
They fly low in giant airplanes
Just to watch the bluebells quake.

Have you ever smelled a meatloaf
As it rises from its bed,
Whether driving to the corner store
Or hanging by a thread?
It can loosen all its juices
As it tightens all its sides;
It will give you all it has to give
And plenty more besides.

Have you ever tasted hunger
In the middle of the night
When all the men and women
Were just itching for a fight?

The children eat and then complain
The meatloaf's too well done,
But we'll only get home safely
If we sail on to the sun.

In The Doghouse

it is cold and lonely
without furniture
but still
the tail wags
out of love

Ladies in Waiting at the Prado

He knew intrigue well, Velazquez did,
Secreted as he was in a clandestine court
Of veiled mistresses and diabolical schemes;
But here and now in these benign halls of marble,
Amid varied works and obscured centuries,
We see the wondrous vision of his meaning
In this simple scene arrayed before us:

The child, the dwarf and the artist
Are perfectly comfortable
Openly staring straight at you,
While you, abstruse to them, even in this bright place,
Are mesmerized by their gaze, barely cognizant
Of the solicitous attendants (one caught in a covert glance),
The mysterious murmurings of the Church,
Or the royal pet casually coopted as a child's footstool.

Only now, as the eye skims the shimmering surface,
Do you espy the furtive figure doorway-framed upon the stairs,
Concealed, initially, through misdirection, as if by a famulus,
And wonder what exactly is he searching for?

As a crowd of ladies from a foreign land press you onward
You surreptitiously turn to their guide's serene gesticulations;
Suddenly, now, transfixed, you see her confidential revelation
Of the purloined letter and unseen Easter egg,
Nearly amorphous but of such obvious power
In the dark glass (blurred and sliced by vague light),
You wonder why such nobility was meant to be disguised.

Though frustrated by inscrutable language, you can still see her
Indicate clearly the precise placement of each of the heads,
To take from their measurement a new, hidden meaning;
And as her hand sweeps in a balletic, upward swoosh,
You behold the preponderance of the artist's design,
Which had always been evident, but simply ignored,
The vast, murky panorama of paintings and ceiling,
A revelation of a shrouded chiaroscuro,
Hinting at still yet another meaning:
An ulterior plan to clasp to itself
The wonder of a new world
Waiting for discovery.

Yet The Day Is So Glorious

The day is so glorious with sunshine and laughter,
The night so cool and so fresh;
We walk, hand in hand,
For as far as we can,
Refusing to think of what surely comes next.

I watch our granddaughter play tennis unable
To believe she will one day be as old as I,
Yet I know this to be true;
Yes she, charging the net with fearless abandon,
May in time endure the arthritic pain
That imbues my body from morning to night.
How is that possible?

Our daughter has entered middle-age,
Still a beauty, 'tis true, but yet,
Like your beauty now, also different;
Our son's hair is grizzled and frayed,
Framing a face lined subtly with care.
This cannot be,
Yet it is.

We are old, my love.
How did it happen so quickly?
It was only yesterday
We were looking for the house
In which to raise our children;
Today, that house is too large,
With far too many stairs.

Sunrise and sunset appear always the same,
With golden and ruby-red grace;
E'en so, we cannot forget that
They're in opposite parts of the sky.

Yet lying in bed, so close and so warm,
In the darkling reaches of night,
We can still choose, if we wish, to remember
The brilliance we shared together at noon.

A Divine Symphony

I. Allegro con brio

"Call me Ishmael"

Retreat!
Retreat!

Blank faces stared out or down to screens
Intent on crowded platforms teens
I see in times of trouble conformed
With coats pressed for shelter in the warmed
But slanted tubes a drafty slice of care
Buried deep within the earth rare
Metals and fibers are all abrade
As whipped by blust'ry snow forayed.

Run to the station
In my abnegation
Of masculation
A tearful perturbation
Get back!

The mind of man is dark and bitter cold
Plunging depths in woeful arcs unforetold
As ash and slime veneer the terrible sheen
Till Zulfiqar and the nine can dare be seen
Thus do such deeply hidden powers tend
To prostrate fears long before my end
In storied layers bent harsh against the bold
Dirge of hours sometime before when I took hold
On wet and perfunctory feet that day
And thus revealed a pungent strip of clay.

Oh baby baby
Don't say maybe
Oh my soul
Black as coal
Oh so nice
Cold as ice
Roll the dice
Dig it!

Hardened ground provided a different way within the hole
Where bundled forms burrowed and like a frightened mole
I'm rescued from the tiller's blackened hand in the reaction
To an unexpectedly fervid rock or stone the satisfaction
Of which a struggle faced and won by my unattended walk
Around the black stone rock from labor's barren stalk
Of maize or soy or kale or some fruit from vine or tree
Whose coarse brown bark shielded the brittle sentry
To a realm where the Prophet stood with legs spread wide
And arms akimbo his piercing eyes through the darkest guide
Had led the teeming masses to a distant time
When all the earth wore the tattered robe of doleful rime.

Train jerked past
Signs blurred fast
Strangers together crammed
On buckled legs damned
To solid ground that cast
Blurred signs passed
Abandoned tracks at last
Ankle-deep and blind
Moving stairs behind
Departing glacier declined
The past unassigned
Never!

She beside me presses within herself a scarf across her face
Like an umber-gilt hijab that lowered her gaze and feared to trace
The wind-swept people cloaked and bowed before the onslaught
Of sunken trogs who once were dearly sold or piously bought
Scurried upon the platform chasing paper like legions of lost deer
Come on baby stay with me now and don't give in to fear
To chance the act in the belly of the beast who spouted long ago
When knees were bent upon the rug that covered a vanquished foe
As I alone gripped the bare stalactites that once were deeply strung
Within the recess where the deaf and blind Neanderthals had clung
In filth and grime to hunker 'gainst dread winter the other clone
Stripped clean and rubbed on ochre shins or shaped with bone
To leave its ruddy mark and scratches 'pon the western wall
The prayer's septum that once I'd climbed before the fall.

Many times I've been alone
Too frozen to atone
As grating metal sounds
Noon's muezzin pounds
Upon the ears of crushed boarders
Boxed like an accursed hoarder's
Chest of clocks and watches from
Clapham Common to Old Street's glum
Reaching Madison or Canal
A frigid earthy bacchanal
'Midst snow so fine
My I me mine
Oh solo me
What can it be
Brimming or bereft
Submerged where nothing's left
Don't leave!

We come to the hajj the way some go to the fridge
Dripping with sweat and fearing the bridge
Over a shapely chasm of despair
We chose instead to stare
Not up but over
And over and over and over
Enduring another lifetime of regret
Our eyes and mouths in grave determination set
I tried to go go go but as yet not yet
Not yet not yet not yet
Pastimes of solitary paternity
Shrink from the onus of maternity
Whilst having peered deep into the darkness of what was
We settled on a frenzied judgement simply because
It wasn't decided as it should have been who
Would be chosen then amongst the few.

How much further I in this horrid wreck must stagger or careen or
  simply tumble blindly
With knees and shins knocked by memories shattered from intentions
  offered kindly
How much longer in this freezing cold must I wallow dread and weary
Feet numb-lost and fretted with sounds muted and sight bleary
It is therefore not without reason we descend once more
To take the IRD or BMT to the Gare du Nord

Or perhaps Pigalle on the Double A
Circle round or I'll have to stay
As weak pins hold no fear
Of the blackened tear
Or a gnarled fate
To another date
But can it wait
Won't it wait
It will wait
Too late
Too late
Too late
Too late.

II. Andante Molto Mosso

"I've heard there was a secret chord that David played and it pleased the Lord."

Nymphs easily recall, as they dilly-dally their gentle promenade
along the trail,
Estuaries and springs of light contrasted with the crocodiles that spill
now from the Nile;
It certainly was so when you and your mother ambled here to seek
what truth is in the tale
Of that from which the gleaming sun provides to those who luxuriate
in the greening of your smile.

'Neath oak and elm she taught you to interpret the lives of the crocus
and the rose
In the languid afternoon as the honeybee and purple martin slowly
make their industrious rounds,
Basking in the light of a warm, cloudless day; a summer's day
like any other, except you chose
This day to work the road of magisterial nature and see and taste
and smell all her sounds.

Now you are here again, with your son, and you lie upon the sloping bank
of the gentle riverside,
Grown gorgeous with lilies and reeds, barely infiltrated
by the great blue heron and its young.
You stare up the trunk of the willow and listen to the rustle of its leaves
on branches hung
In a canopy, like a skullcap on the heart of a young man who beholds
for the first time his tender bride.

But are you really here now? And am I with you? Perhaps not,
but I've seen that road before.
It may have been in my heart's core that I lolled where
the wild thyme and rosemary grow,
Or it may be more like a dream searching for a lullaby. Anyway,
you'll never know;
You must learn the ways of birdsong and the wind by yourself
to discover what's in store.

A million eyes are shaded by the emerald leaves from a million suns
as hands entwine;
The brook is a haven for you and for her, as its fructifying waters are
flowing more freely than wine,

As if the ritual bath of atonement is gently cooled by the east wind
through the shaded wood;
Olive-hued and blond-curled, she splashes, laughing in the water,
on the periphery of womanhood.

Here the child-king is plucked from the bulrush at the river's brink;
here you pass the myrtle shower,
As if phylacteries grasp your arm in friendship and succor you and yours
with the power
Of a rainy day. The sun laughs to lick up the fruits of her clouds as,
now and always now,
At the turning of the road, you perceive the portobello or chanterelle,
the shrub or bough

Projecting selfless tendrils, insufflating spasms in your breast
while you must forego the joy
Of fireworks that claim the sky while the sun recedes. As the children
laugh and weep,
The old women mourn the sparks drowning themselves in the lake,
their whispers coy
To tease the menfolk from the field where, sowing and tilling,
they reap fair love and lavish sleep.

Everybody saw the sunshine from the transept during the beaming solstice,
But now the terpsichorean aphids and gnats crazy grace the air's gloam;
Don't leave me waiting here, perspicacious but still wondering
who would forestall this
Arcane knowledge: the road that stretches out ahead is the only road
to take you home.

Midsummer's day brings all of you out to stare at the blue, blue sky
while you set the water slide
For the children to sport with the pallid martyr. You can celebrate anything
you want, lying in the green,
But only by laying your sons upon the altar of today. Mothers pass
helplessly as their children are seen
Picking violets by the brook, climbing halfway up the tree, or just laughing
with arms thrown wide.

Holding tight your sister's hand, both of you skip through the fresh,
verdant fields of grass,
A barefoot duet upon the fragrant green, replete with the scent
of incense and myrrh,
Gathering chestnuts while you have the time; yes, pet the spaniel,
feel his soft fur

And the frantic beating of his heart, eliding the azure sea, the flinty desert
and the mountain's pass.

Walking further up the road, the giggles of the water stream,
stubborn always, will not cease;
You pass marshland rushes where the gargarey and smew cavort
in a transcendent peace,
But the traygopan averts the length and breadth of the fragrant
meadow's viridian floor.
A pool of tears, like those Mother Miriam shed, form a mournful path
that leads me to your door.

Halfway home by morning, sweet and lovely, still, together,
sacred and longing, but never alone,
Warming yourself by the glowing embers that the commandments
particularly condone,
Nonetheless you must move over; honey dripping from the apple tree's
vibrant hive
Splashes in rivulets of the transient puddle; you sip chartreuse, and, yes,
celebrate those still alive!

So dance, my love, with your ripe breasts bare, and gentle hands
outstretched to catch the sun,
Dance a new dance, when you can, joyful and complete, aching
to be danced when the fast is done;
Sing, my love, with clarion cry, a silver melody that breathes
of riches found and struggles won;
Sing anew, onward, a sauntering croon for the pristine child whose breath
has only just begun....

III. Scherzo and Trio: Presto – Assai meno presto

"Nu ic þē hāte, hæleð mīn se lēofa,
þæt ðū þās gesyhðe secge mannum,
onwrēoh wordum þæt hit is wuldres bēam,
se ðe ælmihtig god on þrōwode
for mancynnes manegum synnum…"

Three abreast will test the best
But they endure it well;
You see those three will be
Sitting by the sun all done;
She will yell but cannot tell
What fell undone for harvest fun
Or when he falls will see
The way that's down is not out;
So shout about and wield the clout
Of rising up up up says the bird
Its beak searching the nest
Above the engines steadily heard;
The rush of the thrush to hush is struggling constantly to make itself
understood.

In whose name do the triplets dance?
Who is speaking words of wisdom in a trance?
Why doesn't the son finally take a chance?

A waltz of leaves she grieves to seize
The canaries that buy the sky
Where they fly and try
To feel the wind blow;
Oh no no no
I told you so
It will not go;
Only crimson leaves will leave the bough;
Only heads upon the bed will bow;
It seems that lemon dreams don't say bye;
No need to try
The orange pie's dye;
Being dead it is said that saffron eyes will surprise as he tries
for this life yet again.

Why do the three of them rattle around so in the mind?
And where in the clouds might they find
A forgiveness that will truly bind?

Vortex of sound looks to fall down;
He found the ground no longer brown
But rather in a slather of blather
Speaking in tongues
Autumnal palaver
On the ladder to climb the rungs
Where there could be absolution;
Tomorrow will borrow the sign;
She will bow her amber lashes
While they cache their stashes
Flying ever higher
Closer to the fire
Where there is nothing left for any of them but an intense longing
for the yellow to be gone.

O Father, who shall it be that I thus offend?
O Son, for whom did you this task intend?
On what rude dream does amnesty depend?

They dare to stare
Riding nowhere
Through the air
Storm-tossed on dross
To bear the cross;
No one cares for such loss
Or for those who'll not
Be shot of the rot
Two millennia bore
To the core
Of this feeling deep inside
That they will abide or hide
When they believe with virtual certainty that, in acquitting them,
he will choose a different life.

Are the equinoctial gales truly a myth?
Whom then will he find himself with?
And will she ultimately be kin or kith?

Look up you sigh
Too late to die
Her tawny hair
Too rare to dare
Too fair to race
Look up for grace
His head's too far
Look to heaven's bar
Look up golden star
Look up cook up
All shook up
Or just look up
Because he promised before he left that he will one day come
to take you home again.

But where is home?

IV. Andante maestoso

"Imagination is the beginning of creation. You imagine what you desire, you will what you imagine and at last you create what you will."

I don't know much about rivers; but I think that those rivers
that flow with such enormity –
As, say, the Amazon or Mississippi – becoming mostly mythic
in proportion, can surely make
Us feel that they convey more than the spring runoff from
the mountains looming so near.

It's been an eternity since we had been home – or at least it seems
like an eternity –
But home is where we are – or were – now, since then,
and this homestead is our stake
If given the opportunity to remain right where we are – or were – now
that we're here.

It's difficult to say what it will be like here – or at least to say it
with any surety –
Especially as we gather in the lower level before we hope to head
out to the lake
For what I imagine is – quite likely – the first time since the thaw
this particular year.

We would light a fire – or try – when the sun goes down and,
under the stars, gaze at the deformity
Of what is – or was – though even exquisite ephemera are no anodyne
for the eternal ache
That binds us – or will bind us – to something we lost or something
we have yet to fear.

Frank traces paired in or up to fold
Bent in shrouded norms of the old
A dash of time to steer the inerrable gleam
Of beveled pieces that stare and dream
Too seldom when profit took sides with dread
And charmed akin the fiercely pried chthonic powers that led
To change or act upon spelunking's spouted shibboleth
Where trees are sent to shrug away each banished breath
Sent down to butt into the clover
And over and over
And over.

Who will it be
Next to me
Right now
Onward!

You should not stay out too long; it will get cold soon, it was not
that late in the season.
You could – of course – go in, to the library where the words
of each generation will surround
You – keeping you warm – and let you hear the nimble knell
of what each poet thought.

You flinch as in a weary wadi all ablaze–fearing that such joy
is treason–
But if you were indeed upon the lake in kayak or canoe,
you'd be aground
By now; so no, the light shall come from elsewhere, or else
it comes for naught.

An oubliette filled with chronometers inadequately hides
the resplendent reason
For the exaggerated expressions of excellence – like a Beethoven
late quartet – you rarely found
When induced by the plenary waves of desire with which
the white-hot fire is fraught.

Up here, however, the kitchen, its blanched walls warmed
by the oven's craft, induces a frisson
Of domestic bliss; the chaff – airborne now – must submit itself
to be barely bound
By vows you took at the vernal tide, so that the quaint quadrille
can be finally taught.

What willow bends and prays the Mi Sheberach in tune
with the gently brimming stream,
Its silver shade dappled on redolent goldenrod, astilbe and yarrow
at its brink; or dream,
Like Jacob, with head upon celestial stone, rising to the bubbling surface,
like silken cream?
The toddler takes your hand, leaning slightly against your thigh,
to be just as she would seem.

The family gathers, as they have before – and will again –
        on worn couches
And chairs; hard athwart, the child, now greatly grown
        to full womanhood,
Fears to see her own children merely as just another car
        in an unending train

To a destination unknown; what a curious creature it is
        that slouches
All the way to a home – in the foyer by now – where no man
        has ever stood
Before, looking to the rebirth of sunshine after the delicious,
        rarefied rain.

Shall they descend or – once again – climb, perhaps to the attic?
        The child grouches
"Why can't you all just make up your mind?"; the overcoat
        of vivacious victimhood
Clings to her dreary dress, against the epistolary tide from
        which she will always strain.

They settle in armchairs of eggshell and wheat – as is their wont –
        their precious pouches
Holding bleached totems of another era, bits of stone and string
        and wood;
From the window we worship the goldfinch, verdin, or loon,
        and their storied refrain.

In haste they race their catholic taste
In milk and meat while the heat of the beat
Sounds a retreat replete
With protest to compel the saffron zest
When the others will rest;
Now grin where the air is thin
As thus they will truly win
The ever-lasting sleep from which they look inside, but entirely now
        without the fear to be awakened.

When is he?
Where will she look up?
Why?

We welcomed the crepuscular contingent when ample ataraxy ripples,
suggestive
Of peace; the dining room table – such as it is – will be laid with cloth
so white
That, reflecting the roseate fire in the grate, it adds
to the season's serenity.

An alabaster tray brings to their table a careful cornucopia made
somewhat restive
By a spritely blessing – given openly, true – that once held enthralled
our sure-fire sight
Of the evening feast in which you passively partake from some
sumptuous spirit of fraternity.

This splendid time is spent congealed by a fragrant moment
of the digestive;
I'd love a dram of port – or a pinch of scotch – to help us finish
off the night
While the eye of love – limpid and alluring – descries, amazed,
the ineluctable quaternity.

They raised that glass of spirits – whichever one you choose –
in an attitude so festive
In my mind I simply cannot comprehend how they could
possibly continue the fight;
After all, you really cannot conceal your souls from the timeless tetrad
of modernity.

Up here, the burden of creation is relieved; the feeling–as always–a little
congestive;
The extra afghan throw upon the bed provides a warmth
evoking a particular perspective
On the most exalted dreams – never to be forgotten –, a phantasmagoria
reflective

Of a pusillanimous anticipation that they fearfully foresaw
as furtive flight
While you, shuffling off the paralysis of a memory – a timorous thought,
lost and slight –
Look to me – such as I am – so that together we may traverse
a future so bright

The splendor cannot be dimmed; we soar – dare we dream –
    o'er roof and tip of tree,
Singing, sailing, darting, dancing, the time, in glory, forever present,
    forever free.
We reach forever at forever, and we gladly tell forever: let it be,
    Let It Be.

TEN SEVEN

I

Dark and light share space and time
In shade and shadow,
Hiding in the crux of consciousness,
Transmuting essence to potency,
Cleaving perception and reality.

They appear and disappear
In a thin pallor, insipid and grey,
A part of yet apart from their conception,
Perplexed by the loss of their purity
(Gravity without mass, song without sonancy,
Dance without movement, love without emotion)
Until the triturated energy of their separation
Fires the particles and waves that, in time, scatter
Throughout the space where light and dark matter.

Unheard and unseen, we listen to and gaze
At the mirific tendrils and mystic rays
That fasten space to time (or time to space)
With the sheer conceit of our desire for grace.
We try to discern the effortless vacuities
In an empty bourne of infinite possibilities
That coalesce, with a singular voice,
Into one last choice.

But there it is again,
The genesis of our light,
Now, within the ambit of a prism
That fractures it with delight,
Dispersing it in celebration
As it abandons the night
To darkness and dreams
As a young woman might,
Secure in her past,
View futures, astounding and bright:
Bestilled in fervor, she sees herself,
A bride arrayed in white,
Choosing, freely and blithely, her groom

(Also formally clad to unite),
As did space with time at mere creation
When nothing became everything
Expanding without cessation
Vanquishing darkness with the light.

But when was that primal moment?
And where, precisely, was that place?
It might have been inevitable
That he asked her to dinner
(Or to a movie or play or even a concert),
Before allure became love
And a life apart became a life together
(As energy became matter).
Yes, it might have been inevitable,
This tender synecdoche of creation:
A choice that was not a choice,
An effort that was effortless,
A love abiding in chaos,
Anarchy seeking order, for example,
In nebulae, galaxies or neutron stars,
To lead us to an overwhelming moment,
Destined perhaps from the beginning
(As if space-time had a beginning),
That endorsed the choice
Of a clear, irrevocable yes.

II

In the beginning there was music,
The mellifluous vibration of strings
(Or air), the aural manifestation of
A mathematical afflatus of space-time;
Random notes congealed into a melody
Singing a singularity into the binary
With a particular dance of pure bliss.

It was order in the midst of chaos
(Or chaos becoming order
In a whirl of primes and their derivatives):
The burst of leptons,
The gesticulations of quarks,

The arias of bosons, photons
And axions, with integrals and angles, acute and obtuse
(Strange equations in the throes of a Hora, Ceilidh or Twist),
Ineluctably integrated into a veridical confabulation
Cascading through a bizarre quanta of celestial myriads
Who charm their way into existence
While phasing in and out of
The euphony of space-time's laws.

Is this where the celebration begins?
In the ecstatic bodies swirling in concentric circles,
Bowing to ellipses or irregular closed loops?
Or perhaps it begins when (with increased
And increasing energy) they crash and break
Into named and nameless conic sections,
Kicking and leaping to the ever-accelerating expansion
Of the ubiquitous musical expression.

The meal is prepared and,
Increasing the celebration, ready to serve,
A pleasing aroma mixing with the sweet suspirations
Of those whose idea is to prolong the dance,
Lifting both bride and groom
To the reality of a heaven conceived
By the consummation of the marriage
Of matter and energy
At the inauguration of the world.

Only now do we deem it inevitable that
The stochastic speculations in that initial melody
(As it modulates through
The infinite numbers beyond the binary
From prime to prime and prime plus prime
As space-time hummed in its own consciousness,
The natality of stars in the universal creche)
Would also birth laws, separate from the First Law,
Long before the knowledge of man
When he counted on fingers
(As one does commandments)
To keep track of the weeks and days
For sacrifices to an avaricious god
Who floats on the periphery of perception
Like a dream of hymns, fluted or chanted

In ancient modes, vaguely remembered,
Pleasing without being pleased,
Challenged without being challenging,
Expressive without being expressed
By original phrasings in ardent measures
Of the inevitable coda.

It was not inevitable, however,
But rather a scintilla of fortune
That such love might yield,
Amongst the abundant descendants
Of space-time, an insalubrious child
Whose coarse cacophony grates
On the parents' apparent passion for order,
Where possibility is frozen into choice.

So there they are,
Forever explaining to the wretch,
Caught in a dissonance they did not choose
(And would not have chosen),
That life begins and ends
In a game of chance and change, which,
Played and danced in a heartful way,
Could raise them all to a harmonious reality
(Perceived as such amongst the stars),
If they would so choose.

III

By all accounts the day would be fair,
Clement with a desert breeze
To be warmed by the sun's arc
Just beginning in the east.
By all reckoning that fragrant air
Would soon be gushing with song,
Even as the still, dark night evolves to morning.
The cries of celebration would be heard
By the young and the old (and those in between),
As their bodies awaken with music,
Lifting their souls to the mountain
Where the Law was given and received.

But today is a remembrance, too,
Of a sacred time in a sacred place,
Abode by laws created, in a moment,
Long before the Law was given.
Today is that day, celebrating
The idea of giving and receiving.
Today is that day that established order,
Replacing what might have been
With what is.

With ringlets bedecked with flowers,
They held hands and danced.
With smiles and tears,
They held each other's eyes, fearlessly,
As the sun dazzled.
They sang and they danced,
Far from the city's tumult,
The placid order of the suburbs,
Or the tepid frenzy of the town's bazaar
Where the feast's luscious ingredients were purchased
And blended to a savory repast
In which all would partake.

Indifferent to outside perception,
They rejoiced, with the bold legerity of youth,
On the love that brought them together,
A love of self devoid of self, immaculate and
Concentered on the other who is the self,
The binary which becomes the singularity,
Only in love.

IV

They came, oddly, from the west.

With time enough to spare, they covered the space
Between civilization and savagery in an instant. They arrived
In the valley where the mountains to the east and the west
Form a choice, offered long ago in the desert,
A choice each generation must make in its time
As each of us must make in our own heart.

But in this space
There would be no time
And at this time
There is no space to abide.
Midst light and dark
Lay doubt and fear
(Transversing accord).
The creation of light
Did not dispel
The choice of darkness.

V

Where does evil sleep?
Does she toss and turn alone on a makeshift bed,
Her attenuated and malignant womb
Bearing mixed multitudes
As she suckles them with her acrid colostrum?

No.

She lies, instead,
On a luxurious mattress, pillowed by down,
Blanketed with sable, warmed by decay,
While waited on by a seemingly infinite
Horde of avid servants,
Nursed with brittle cold and brutal heat
In a squalid hearth of primeval contempt.
Gorging on a feast of ashes, devoid of remorse,
Coiled in deceit, filthy with despise,
Thewless with the elusion of all that is fair,
And wallowing in the malodorous retch that is
The malicious consummation of consentient cruelty,
She rises,
Ready to sacrifice all who are born
(And all those yet to be born)
On a gambit designed to bring the world to its knees.

And so, withershins, they came,
Drunk with revenge and quaking with fury
Over insubstantial grievances and factitious griefs,
Over specious perceptions of injustice and ruin,

Over roads of hate and through tunnels of war,
In motorized vehicles, on heavily shod feet,
And gliding through the air like a murder of crows
Swooping to earth as phlogiston and sulfur,
Destroying all they survey. With twisted minds
And tortuous souls, with lustful violence
And rapacious wrath, seeking no solace,
Boasting no virtues, harboring no ruth,
And granting no quarter, they perpetrated
Such heartless brutality
In a space so small and a time so short
They seemed like the destroyer of worlds.

It happened,
On this day, today, of all days;
The day that broke the vessel
That scattered the sparks
That illuminate the world
Transformed into
The day that broke our hearts
That bled into the sand
That stretches away
Into the dark corners
Of space-time.

That sand is stained with a crimson blot
That cannot be cleansed or edulcorated.
It is an incarnadine vastness,
A dying sun with a heart of rust
In the bitter center of a cold galaxy.

This is, indeed, our scholastic belief,
Promulgated intensely as others fear to opine:
That the day is dark as night and light is as darkness,
That the law is a falsehood to be hated and detested,
That the consciousness in the heart of man is evil,
That there are places where goodness and mercy do not follow,
That there are times when the repentant do not repent,
That there is a space that space itself does not inhabit.

The desert inherits the blood
Of villains and martyrs alike.
It always has and always will:

That is the law of the desert.
The very idea of it haunts our vision
And audition, extending, as it does,
From infinite possibility to the singular choice
Of granting to all fair music and light,
Both gifts now vitiated
By discord and the dark.

(We are all hostages to space-time.)

VI

Dawn blushes, Spring blinks,
Day sighs, Summer sleeps,
Evening rushes, Autumn slinks,
Night cries while Winter weeps.

He kneels at the graveside of his beloved
(A lifetime whisked away in an instant),
His perception of reality dimmed,
Conscious only of a limitless ache.
Children beside him, and children of children
(As well as children unborn
And children who will never be born),
He wonders how it will all end, or if it will end,
While his bride is interred in motley and his tears
Flood a meaningless moment.
He knows that life will go on, but
Only because it has no choice
But to go on.

VII

As there is architecture in Space,
The spectacular houses erected on behalf of the gods,
The commodious homes designed by the rich for the rich,
The ziggurats planted amongst the slums in the center of cities,
A canopy of gossamer silver swaying over bride and groom,
An opera house that seems to defy the laws of gravity,
A museum or mausoleum whose floors mirror
The echo of clacking footfalls and whose ceilings descry

The attenuating memories housed in its vaults and crypts
Or hanging on its walls,
So too are there structures wrought in Time,
Each conceived with a love of the sublime,
Diffusing its own luster and heaving its own shadows
Of our celebrations, events, regrets and woes,
The entirety of which (this sweeping progression of moments:
Concentric, iterative, vortical rhythms whose components
Of hours, months, seasons or jubilees,
Stretch, even with all of our difficulties,
From attoseconds to eons and beyond),
Having begun when intrinsic energy mattered the most
(That instant the primordial particles spawned
From the initial fissure of space-time, the host
Of the universe), passes inexorably from prime to prime
In a threnody to the inevitable entropic demise of all,
When there is no space and there is no time
To hold both light and dark in thrall;
And still the Law abides, unseen and unheard,
To establish that evil, by love, will be cured
And that man shall wage war
No more.

About the Author

To learn more about the author, please email him at gryphonandlyre@gmail.com.

www.ingramcontent.com/pod-product-compliance
Lightning Source LLC
Chambersburg PA
CBHW040529170726
48295CB00012B/390
* 9 7 8 1 9 5 8 4 1 1 1 2 4 *